About the Author

Precious Dikko wrote her first book when she was nine years
old and has been writing ever since. She's lived in three
different countries on two continents, but now resides in
Dublin with her family.
"To Catch a Rebel" is her debut novel.

To Catch a Rebel

Precious Dikko

To Catch a Rebel

Olympia Publishers
London

www.olympiapublishers.com
OLYMPIA PAPERBACK EDITION

A CIP catalogue record for this title is
available from the British Library.

ISBN: 978-1-78830-595-2

This is a work of fiction.
Names, characters, places and incidents originate from the writer's
imagination. Any resemblance to actual persons, living or dead, is
purely coincidental.

First Published in 2020

**Olympia Publishers
Tallis House
2 Tallis Street
London
EC4Y 0AB**

Printed in Great Britain

Acknowledgements

Thank God for words and perseverance both without which, *To Catch a Rebel* wouldn't have been possible. Thanks, Mom for your love and support and for letting me hog the laptop hours on end. I love you.

Thank you Lynda Nì Chealleachàin for reading the first draft and giving up class time to give us all vital life lessons. You are a star.

Thank you, Mr Dockery for making us read young adult literature for our Leaving Cert.

Thank you, James Houghton, and all the editors at Olympia publishing London, for seeing potential in my summer project and making it even better. Thank you, Kristina Smith, Megan Whiting, and the rest of the production department for all the work that you do.

Thank you, Kiera Cass, Soman Chainani, Tomi Adeymi, Victoria Aveyard, Marissa Meyer, Ni Chealleacháin and Kathryn Stockett for great reading material and everything I have learnt about storytelling. Last but not least, thank you, the readers, especially those who came to the end of the acknowledgements. You sure are diligent.

Chapter 1

I heard the news that morning. More than half the nation was in mourning because the King of Xavia had passed away in the night. In other words, my father passed away.

The king's guards had arrived at our door at around six. They took me into the kitchen and told me what happened; it had been in his sleep. The doctors were called and tried to do everything they could, but it was too late. His heart had stopped. They offered their condolences and allowed Ma Osa, her daughters, and David, my personal guard, to come in and see me. Ma Osa, my foster mother took me in her arms holding me; Judith and Winter held my hands and stroked my hair while David talked silently to the other guards who were looking nervously in my direction.

In all of this, I didn't seem to feel anything. Sure, there were a few tears in my eyes from the shock of it all, but they quickly disappeared. I suppose you can't feel that much about a person who you haven't seen in almost ten years.

"Your mother wished to come and tell you," said one of the guards fiddling with a letter in his hand. "But she realized the danger."

I nodded in understanding. These were dangerous times. Even more so now after what had happened. He handed the card to me, his eyes filled with sympathy. Now the tears began to surface.

"I want to read it alone please," I breathed, holding the letter to my chest.

"Of course, Your Highness," replied the guard, bowing, and nodded to his partner to leave with him. Your Highness. I hadn't heard that in ages, but I recognized the writing on the card instantly. I'd seen it so many times before. I turned around and saw that I was alone. They were all in the sitting room.

I heaved in a breath and sat down on a stool. I traced the cursive writing on the envelope, tore it open then pulled out the letter...

To my dearest Imotenya,

By the time you get this, you will have probably heard the news about your father. I'm so sorry you couldn't be at his side during his final moments, but you know how the situation is. Why you couldn't be with us in the first place. He spoke of nothing but you. I know from your letters that Ma Osa is treating you very well and that David is keeping a firm eye on you, but it's time for you to come home now. I wish I could put it off, but the advisors said that we demonstrate a show of power to the rebels.

I froze at the mention of the rebels. The reason why I couldn't be with my family. The reason why this kingdom was in turmoil. I swallowed then continued with the letter...

They need to see that the kingdom's new hope is unafraid. I'm so worried though. They were as far as the city just last week and if they breach the palace, God knows what could happen.

But I hope for the best and count my blessings. I will get to see you again. I suppose you've grown so beautiful. Will you still recognize your dear Mama? I've entrusted you to the king's own guards for protection and, of course, you have David for your journey to the palace. Have a safe journey home my love, and I'll see you soon. I love you.

From Mother

That's when the floodgates opened. I pushed it clumsily back into the envelope for fear that my tears would wash off the ink. I loved my mother and from what I read from her letters, she loved me too, but did she know me? I hadn't seen her or the palace in almost ten years, not counting the time Ma Osa took us to Beni City for the annual parade near the palace.

Ma Osa, Judith, Winter. They were the only real family I'd known for most of my life. This was the only life I'd known. Now I'd have to leave it for some palace under threat to take a role that I wasn't even sure I was prepared to take.

"Aria?" I turned to see David peering round the door. "We need to speak with you." I certainly did not want to speak to them. I already knew what they were about to say.

"We have to leave now," I said, "Don't we?" My guard's silence spoke volumes. "Well tell them we're not going."

"Ria, we have to…"

"No, we don't!" I snapped, locking eyes with him. He made a few steps towards me and reached for my shoulders; a gesture that always seemed to quell me out of my foulest of moods, but not today. I jerked back almost falling off my stool. "Have you not heard of the threats in and around the palace and you all want to throw me into all that!"

"Aria, the kingdom needs you!" David yelled back. Then

he backed away slightly. I was a little stunned at that outburst. Not because, I outranked him but because there were only two times when he really yelled at me. Once was when I laid down in the middle of the road and tried to see how quickly I could get up before I got ran over. The second time was when I almost stabbed myself while fiddling with a ceremonial sword. The things those two had in common was that I was doing something really stupid.

He took a breath and ran a hand quickly through his short hair. "I'm sorry, Your Highness," he said calmly. "But people everywhere are worried. Right now, nobody is sure who the heir is. Many believe you're dead."

I shivered. And many more want me dead.

"They need to see that stability can resume for the kingdom. They need to see that there's hope for us still." Hope. New hope. That's what my mother had called me in her letter. That's what I had to be. It was my duty. Whether I wanted it or not.

I sighed and got up. "Okay. We'll go."

David looked relieved as if he knew that if I didn't agree, he would have to drag me out of the house pulling and screaming until we got to the palace.

"Hey," he whispered, stooping down to my level which even at 15 going on 16 was quite low. "Security has been increased and I'll be with you just as I have been all these years, little dove." I chuckled a little. That endearment, which to me was an oxymoron, was a favourite of David's from the moment when I was thrust into his arms for protection at age five. I began to feel a bit guilty. For all my tantrums, stubbornness and rebellious nature, David had always been by my side. A part of me knew that this was his duty as a guard, but another part felt like he actually liked me. Not as a monarch, or protectorate, but as a friend.

He smiled too, but then his expression grew slightly sombre. "I'm sorry about your father," he said looking truly sorry for me. "And I'm sorry that I'm only telling you that now." I chuckled again.

"It's all right, you had things to discuss. I understand." He nodded and moved to hug me, but the kitchen door opened with the guard almost falling in.

"Your Highness," he breathed quickly. "It is best that we leave as soon as possible."

David and I nodded and made our way out to where Judith and Winter were sweeping and Ma Osa was sitting down, but got up once she saw me. She looked stricken. I ran into her arms again, my face pressed against her chest. I hadn't even considered how Ma Osa would feel at my leaving. She basically raised me alongside her own children. She was strong, so loving, I almost felt bad at leaving. I turned to the door and saw Judith and Winter standing there, brooms in hand, with the same expression as their mother. Ma Osa let go of me and dried her eyes with the edge of her apron.

"Winnie, find a bag for Aria." Winter ran in towards the cupboard while Judith came in and pushed me towards the bathroom.

"Wash quickly," she said then made her way to our shared bedroom.

I brushed my teeth and poured water from the shower into the bucket. It was cold as we didn't have time to boil water. Not many had hot water in Sapele. I used a bowl to splash water over my body. I wanted to forgo the soap, but then I remembered I was going to the palace. I suppose I was to make a decent impression. I got out and wrapped myself in the nearest towel then rushed to our bedroom.

Judith and Winter were there; Judith pulling out some of my clothes and Winter holding an old suitcase. "Winnie, you found it," I gasped looking at the little black thing. It was the same suitcase that I brought with me ten years ago.

"Yes," giggled Winter. "I'm sure it can hold everything you have." That was a no-brainer. I had a scarce number of clothes, some trinkets and a few books on politics and history that I had never read. "I can't believe you're going to the palace!" she continued excitedly.

"Of course, she is," snapped Judith. "It's where her family is."

I pulled Winter towards me softly, taking in her bright eyes and removing some dust from her short hair. She was a sweet little thing and was just a baby when I first met her.

"We're your family too," she said indignantly looking at Judith then turned back to me with her wide eyes. "Right?"

I laughed. "Yes, you are. You're the daughter of my mother's father's third wife's sister's daughter."

"And what's that in English?" sniffed Judith suppressing a smile. She had seemed so cold and grown up in the last few years so I was glad when she still engaged in our inside jokes.

There was a knock on our door. Winter answered and Ma Osa stepped in. "Are you finished?" she asked and noticed our sheepish expressions and the empty suitcase. She just ignored us and I noticed she had a clothing wrap.

"It's for you Aria."

I took it, unzipped it and gasped at what I saw. It was a black dress — a mourning dress.

I sighed a little. I had almost forgotten the actual reason I had to go to the palace. I fingered the black tulle that billowed at the ends with velvet roses at the sleeves.

"It's beautiful," whispered Judith. "Even though it's black." Winter stared at the dress utterly awestruck. It was probably the most opulent thing she had ever seen in her life and this was just a mourning dress. I put it on and relished the feel of it against my skin. Ma Osa, Judith, and Winter looked at me sweetly.

"You look like a princess," she said, rushing to hug me.

"No, my dear," said Ma Osa fondly. "She is a princess."

Chapter 2

I didn't really have to pack anything as I'd be measured for new clothes when we got to the palace and all the books and other things I might need would be provided, but I packed a scarf given to me by Ma Osa, my bundle of letters, and my sun necklace, a gift from my mother. Ma Osa had packed me some food for the journey as well.

I dragged my suitcase out with the help of Judith as Winter came out behind us.

We were met with a limousine flanked by two Bentleys. We gasped. Even though I came here in a limousine, I was still thrilled to see one right outside my door. The guards stood by one Bentley and David against the other. It brought back how real the situation was now. I turned to my foster family. They embraced me in an intimate hug that I didn't want to leave. We pulled back eventually, but Winter held onto my hand.

"Promise me," she whimpered. "That you'll write, tell me everything won't you?"

"I will," I said to her and to Judith who tried to hide the tears in her eyes. She, like her mother, was tough. She squeezed my shoulder and bent down towards my ear, her braids brushing my cheek. "I'm sure you can do it," she whispered. "Be a princess, I mean."

My shoulders tensed a bit. "I hope so." She let go of me and smiled.

I moved towards the car giving the driver my suitcase then looked at the house that had been my home all these years. The small windows with the homemade curtains, the soot-stained walls, the stray nails that stuck out at odd places and the small grasses that grew by the doorway. I'd miss this place.

"Your Highness." I heard a voice behind me. It was the driver holding open the door of the limo to me. I breathed slowly. Here we go. I stepped into the limo and David slid into the seats opposite me. They were made of soft black leather with golden threads. I looked out the window and watched my foster family waving at me. I waved back as the driver slipped into his seat and the guards got into their car.

We began to drive out of the compound while Winnie ran after the limo, her little legs looking like they were flying until she and the house and Judy and Ma Osa were far in the distance, but I continued waving as if that would keep them closer. We drove through the sandy streets where shops were starting to open and people were sweeping their storefronts and the fronts of houses. Some people looked up and gave us some waves and cheers at the prospect of seeing a royal entourage. It was probably the most interesting thing they'd seen since palm wine. A man in a wrapper, with a toothbrush still in his mouth, came running out of a backyard shouting after us. "Long live the king."

I sighed sadly. Did anyone else not know yet?

"I don't think the newspapers have been sent out," said David, probably reading my mind. "Besides, it's Sapele, they'd probably be the last to know if the world was ending."

I laughed. That was true. If not because of my distant

family being here, Sapele was a good place to hide. It was a small rural village where everyone was happy in their small corner of the world and almost could afford to be oblivious to what went on the other side of the 'Goodbye Sapele' sign that we had just passed.

"There is bread and mineral in the cooler," the driver said, looking at us through the mirror.

"Thank you," I replied remembering that we had skipped breakfast. He smiled, putting up the glass between the driver's seat and the passenger seats.

I pulled a small lever and out popped a selection of fizzy drinks and bottles of water. I took a bottle that said 'sparkling water' then looked at David staring pensively out the window then took out another one.

"Here," I offered him the bottle. He took it silently with a grin.

"Thank you, Your Highness."

I sighed. "It's just me."

"Well, it won't be when we're at the palace, so we better start getting used to it." That alerted me to something.

"You'll still be my guard, right?"

"Of course," he answered as if it was the most obvious thing in the world. "It's what I was trained to do wasn't it?"

"Was herding cattle and farming part of your training too?" I quipped.

While in Sapele, David had worked on our neighbour's small plot of land to be close to me. "Not really," he shrugged. "Just something I picked up along life."

David's family was well off enough and I think was in business, not agriculture. That job was reserved for him as the youngest of eight brothers. Most of them went into the business field while others joined the army. David was only fourteen as he'd told me when he arrived at the palace to train for a place in the Guards. After a few months, he got assigned to be my guard. He had confided to me himself on how he didn't understand why I was not assigned someone older and more experienced, but he said that with what he had demonstrated, he was the best candidate not even mentioning the fact he would not be recognized as being from the palace.

The road was wide and open with an abundance of trees and red sand, hitting potholes constantly. We passed the tiny village of Mosalgar where we had gone swimming last summer. Ma Osa's oldest son Koda came as well with his wife and children, and Uncle Philip; we made a whole day of it. I began to feel nostalgic. With all the prestige at the palace, would I be happy there?

"David, did you like being at the palace?" I asked, looking at him intently. He turned to me and smiled. "You've lived there for five years," he said but then his face fell a bit when he saw my expression. "You don't remember it?"

"Not really. We don't talk about it that much," I said. "But I suppose things would have changed by now anyway."

"You're right," he replied. "Unless the rebel attacks have been understated."

"Have you ever been involved with the rebels?" David bit his lip and looked out the window again.

"Yes. There were attacks when we were there. Ever since the law change." The law change. Where all our problems began.

Ever since the start of the monarchy, only a male heir could take the throne. That's why in the past, kings had many wives to increase the chance of having a boy. When I was born, my mother demanded that the law be changed. She thought it unfair that because of my gender I'd lose my birth right. There were a lot of disputes and agreements but, eventually, Princess Imotenya Aria Accra was the heir apparent.

Of course, this revolutionary action split the nation. Literally. Many Chiefs left the council and started rebellions against all that Xavia stands for; not to mention the nearest male relative, my Uncle Lucky that was cheated out of his chance of the crown. So, basically, my so-called birth right had put a blazing target on my back especially after the time my nursery in the palace mysteriously caught on fire. Everyone suspected it was Uncle Lucky. That was why I had to live away from the palace. For my own protection. Until today.

I was starting to feel a little sleepy even though at this time of the day everyone would be awake.

"You can lie down if you want," said David kindly, pulling out a blanket from another compartment.

"Can I move next to you?" I asked, looking earnestly. David didn't look so sure at this. "I don't think that would be appropriate…"

"Please."

He pursed his lips then motioned to the seat next to him. I took off my seatbelt and moved beside him. I leaned my head against his shoulder as I had done so many times before and he tucked the blanket up to my neck. Soon after that, I fell asleep.

Chapter 3

"Ria? We're almost there."

My eyelids fluttered at the sound of David's voice. He removed his arm that had been around my shoulder for a while and that was enough to prompt me to sit up, the blanket falling to the floor.

I looked out and saw that we had finally entered Beni City. The sand was redder, the buildings were taller and everything seemed much more elaborate. As we drove through the city, I sensed a sombre atmosphere throughout. I caught sight of some newspaper vendors. The story must be out now. The king's death. We drove past the Oba's market and the museum then there it was.

The palace.

It's high orange gates stood out amongst the cream walls. There were golden images of lions along some of the walls. The gates opened and we drove inside. I saw that the sand inside the gates seemed lighter than that on the Beni roads. There were other buildings inside the grounds as well. I recognized them vaguely from what I saw on TV and from memory.

There was the administrative building to the left where all the offices were and where the king received visitors, and in the past made judgments.

Further down was a post office, a school, and even a zoo. I wondered if I had been raised in the palace, would that school be where I got my education.

We came to a space that was bound off by red rope marked 'Royal'. The other car stopped in a space beside us. The driver got out and opened the back door.

"Your Highness," he bowed with an outstretched hand. I took it. This would take some getting used to. David followed and looked around cautiously. Once he was sure we were safe, he nodded to the driver.

"Have a good day Your Highness," he said with a humble smile.

"And to you," I replied. With that, he walked towards the direction of the administration chambers.

The other guards had gotten out as well and were standing still as if awaiting orders.

"Let's go," David said authoritatively to the guards. Without a word, they positioned themselves right in front of us and we moved in the direction of what I remembered as the royal family living quarters. My new home.

Two bronze lions were perched on either side of the door, bronze being our country's national stone. Inside there was an abundance of silver ornaments as well as wooden masks, ivory tusks and ornate jewellery pieces. If this was the main hall, I wondered what the actual rooms would look like. Some guards were on patrol through the hall and a few maids were sweeping and polishing the décor, but all activity seemed to halt as soon as they saw me. The maids bowed down low and some of the guards saluted. It felt strange being in a room where everyone was paying homage to me. I just smiled and followed the two guards in front of me. I heard a maid behind me say, "She's so little," while another hummed in agreement. I wanted to turn around, but then thought that would make things more nerve-wracking than they were already.

We approached a parlour at the end of the corridor. Potted hibiscus stood on either side and I could hear the sound of chatter from inside. I turned to David and he gave me a look saying 'it's all right'.

One guard knocked at the door and an almost inaudible 'enter' came. He pushed open the door and he stepped inside saying, "My queen, she's here."

He gestured for us to follow him when he and his partner stood on either side of the door as if they were there the whole time.

The room was not as embellished as the main hall, but there was a touch of class that made you stare in awe. But I didn't. I didn't because standing in front of me was a woman in a black dress like mine only more ornate. Her hair was held up by black beads that under normal circumstances would be a deep orange.

A silence passed between us before she ran to hug me.

"Imotenya," she whispered, her voice breaking, holding me tight. "You're home."

I breathed in her soft vanilla scent and exquisite soap that put my homemade lump to shame.

"Hello Mother," I squeaked into her shoulder, relishing this moment. Sure, Ma Osa gave me hugs occasionally, but it wasn't the same as having the person who gave birth to you — who was meant to love you unconditionally — hug you. It just felt natural even if you hadn't seen them in almost forever.

She pulled back almost reluctantly as if realizing that we were not alone. She caught sight of David and reached out for his hand. He came over and went down on one knee reverently. "Thank you," Mother said, sounding more queen-like. "For my daughter."

He just bowed his head in such a humble and sweet manner.

"It was my honour to be of service to the king," he replied then looked at me. "And to be in the company of such a charming young girl."

I would have blushed if my checks were light enough.

Mother just nodded and gestured for the guards, and David got up to leave.

"David, wait," I called before he could walk out the door. He turned and I walked towards him tentatively. I really wanted to hug him, but felt like that wouldn't be professional for both of us.

"Tell me I'll see you around soon," I pressed. I might have had my mother, but that didn't mean I wouldn't want a more familiar face around.

He raised an eyebrow. "What will you do if you don't?"

"Something drastic."

"Then you will, little dove." He gave me a wink and one final bow to the queen and left the room.

I turned to my mother who was seated on a chaise. I noticed that there were two other women in the room who had remained silent throughout our reunion. One sat on a stool dressed in mourning robes that almost swallowed her up. Tiny glasses were perched on her nose and she was sewing what looked like a quilt. The other seemed about my mother's age also in black clothing, but hers was more form-fitting and would be suitable for everyday use if the colour black wasn't banned at the palace. She smiled at me with a glass in her hand.

"So, is this her?" she said putting her glass down, and came up to me giving me a hug. Who was she? I didn't recognize her at all.

"Welcome home, my dear," she said kissing my cheeks. I stepped back a little. "You don't remember me, do you?" She smiled cheerfully dragging me to the chaise Mother had gotten up from.

"How could she?" gruffed the other woman, still not looking up from her work, "She was still being carried when she last was here."

So Madam Smile and Madam Quilt somehow knew me when I was last here.

Mother sat down next to me while Madam Smile took a sip from her glass.

"Imotenya," she said stroking my hair. "These are your aunties."

She pointed to Madam Quilt and introduced 'Auntie Osoye' who just grunted, turning over her quilt. She gestured to Madam Smile and said: "Auntie Ayela," who grinned taking a longer sip of her drink that I began to notice was wine. Maybe that was what was causing her to smile so much under the circumstances.

"So," my Mother began. "How was your journey, my love?"

"To be honest, I was asleep for most of it."

"Eh? You didn't eat?" Auntie Ayela squeaked, raising her hand and spilling her drink. "She must have something!"

As if on cue, my stomach growled before Auntie Ayela stepped into the hallway shouting: "Maid, maid! Ask the kitchen to make lunch!"

She flounced back in and sat down, eventually, on another stool that was positioned right beside me. There was something on my mind that had been nagging on me from the moment I stepped into the palace.

"Mama, Baba is he...?"

She stiffened slightly and looked away from me.

"He's been washed, but he's still in his room," said Auntie Osoye solemnly, looking at me with a sorry expression; the only bit of emotion I had seen in her so far.

"Can I see him?" I asked, already getting up. Mother tried to hold me back. "I don't think so. Not after your journey."

"Please, Mama."

My aunties were giving her the same imploring look. She sighed and took my hand. My aunties got up in respect as my mother and I left the room. We went up the stairs to the third floor where the royal chambers stood. A red rug was on the ground, its tone contrasting the ombre colour of the walls. It was beautiful.

As we came to Baba's room, a line of guards stood outside their brown khaki pants and red shirts similar to those worn by the guards that brought me to the palace.

They nodded solemnly in turn before we went inside.

The room was huge: king-sized, as I expected, with a large dining table and a rifle cabinet on the wall. A large canopy bed stood in the middle where my father lay.

He was wearing a white agbada which was sewn with gold and green threads. There were emerald beads around his neck with a gold pendant at his chest. There was a white hat on his head and the simple brown sandals on his feet gave off an old-school vibe.

He looked so regal. So strong. Even in death.

I couldn't stop myself. I wanted to be strong and if I couldn't be, at least I should look strong like Baba always did.

But I couldn't.

Instead, I wept. I clung to the bedpost as Mother came over and held me. I heard her own muffled sobs as she whispered, "It's all right, it's all right. We're going to be fine."

'We're'.

In all this, I hadn't even considered how she must be feeling right now. She'd lost her husband at a time of complete uproar. She needed me almost as much as the kingdom did.

I wouldn't think of the kingdom or the rebels or anything right now. All that mattered now was being here to support my family.

Chapter 4

Lunch was in the dining room. The one in the living quarters that was only used for members of the royal family and close personal guests.

To be honest, I don't remember ever being in this room. Perhaps I was too young to sit at a table, which I wouldn't find hard to believe. Even now, I still prefer something quick rather than actually sitting down for a meal, but that didn't mean that I wasn't absolutely relishing the egusi soup and iyan.

I always took part in making meals in Sapele. I knew that the fluffy clumps were the main attraction in egusi so that's why I always added egg whites and fried the seeds beforehand. Another thing I'd miss about Sapele was cooking. Here, there were servants for that.

"How is Ma Osa?" Mother asked, causing me to drop my freshly rolled iyan into the soup.

"They're well," I replied. "But they seemed sad that I had to leave so soon."

"They're sad because of the money they're losing so soon," scoffed Auntie Osoye, taking a sip of water. "They're not expecting more, I hope, now that the girl is gone."

"Money?" I asked.

"You think taking care of royalty is cheap? If you couldn't live in the palace you might as well have certain standards."

"They spent the money on you right?" Mother asked worriedly. "They didn't use it to buy stock for that shop of theirs?"

"No." Not that I had a clue. As far as I was concerned, I had three meals a day, had clothes on my back and had weekly tutoring sessions. I was satisfied.

"When's the burial?" I questioned Mother, determined to change the topic from my foster family.

"I haven't organized that yet," she said and I could see a few tears at the corner of her eye and almost felt guilty. "But I suppose it will be sometime next month."

I nodded and we continued the rest of the meal in silence, Auntie Ayela getting tired of wine and downing water.

"Would it be all right to go to my room to rest for a bit?" I asked my mother.

"Of course," she said. "I'll take you there myself."

She got up from her seat, my aunties and I followed. I wondered what it was like having your every step mimicked by those deemed beneath you.

My aunties went back to the sitting room while my mother and I went back upstairs.

Winter always wanted to live in a house with a staircase so she could slide down on it like they do in those old movies. I'd have to include the staircase in any letters I'd write to her.

We were on the third floor and we came to a mahogany door.

"Here we are," Mama announced opening the door and my mouth dropped open. I thought baba's room was large but this was mine.

A large bed stood at the corner with a lampstand on either

side. A set of double doors which led to the balcony was at the right. I had a desk and table with an adjacent bookshelf.

The room had a bathroom as well as an actual bath.

Forgetting all decorum, I ran inside and opened a red tap. I couldn't believe it.

Hot water from the tap! I laughed looking around at the water closet and the cabinet above the sink. Most people in Sapele used a room with a hole in the ground and even if they had a toilet, it was broken. I tried this one and the swirling water astounded me.

Grinning like an idiot, I turned to my mother who just smiled sadly. "Oh, Imotenya, you would have had so much."

"I have so much already," I bounded back into the room. I'm definitely including this room in my letters.

"It was only cleaned a few days ago but if you want to change anything, the paint, the bed you just ask your maids."

"My maids?"

Mother turned as if forgetting something and pressed a button near the door. No sooner had she done that, three girls scurried into the room bowing before the queen.

"Ma'am," they greeted in unison.

"Imotenya," Mother began. "These are your maids, Hanna…"

She pointed to the one whose hair was tied in a bun and her face boasted years of experience who, for some reason, I seemed to recognize.

"She was your nanny when you were here," said Mama fondly.

I looked at Hanna's adoring eyes and it clicked. She was the one who tried to put me to bed and tried her best to read me stories even though, I think, she was illiterate. I smiled at her warmly.

"Miracle…," Mama continued and pointed to a pretty girl with braids who seemed to bounce on her feet.

"And Petal."

She pointed to a slight thing with a measuring tape in her hand who smiled shyly at me.

"We were working on her Highness's new wardrobe ma'am," said Hanna. "But we didn't know her size…"

"But we found some temporary outfits," interrupted Miracle brightly and she bounced to the wardrobe.

Some was a bit of an understatement. Sure a few of the outfits were black for the mourning period, but there were brightly coloured blouses and flowing skirts and a couple of dresses. There was a drawer for shoes which were some version of heels and even one for jewellery, namely the ceremonial orange beads. I was so entranced by it all that I almost didn't hear Petal's tiny, "Your Highness? May I take your measurements please?"

I shrugged, "Sure."

She nodded holding out the measuring tape around my waist, along my shoulders and arms and then measured my height all the while calling out the numbers to Hanna who jotted them down in her notebook while Miracle re-arranged the pillows on the bed. These girls seemed to be very familiar with their work here.

"Okay, we're done," said Petal, placing the tape measure in the pocket of her uniform. Mother got up from her place at my desk and came to kiss me on the forehead.

"I'll see you later my dear," she whispered, stroking my hair then inspecting the unruly curls. "Something will have to be done with your hair of course."

I wrinkled my nose at that. My hair seemed fine to me if it was a little long. It was Mother who was so opposed to me having it cut in the first place. I felt like a Nazarite.

"We'll come up with something, Your Majesty," said Hanna looking over my hair picturing what would suit me.

"Well I should get back to work," Mama announced walking towards the door. "I will come to check on you later, but your maids will assist you with anything you need."

"Thank you, Mother," I said, getting onto my bed. So it didn't just look soft.

Mother smiled and left down the hall leaving me alone with my maids. They were just standing there patiently and I had almost forgotten that they were probably expecting me to order them around.

"Is the room to your satisfaction Princess?" asked Hanna.

"Yes, it's perfect," I replied, relishing the silken sheets.

"Would you like to change into something more comfortable Princess?" questioned Miracle already making a beeline for the wardrobe.

"No, I'm all right."

"Is there anything else you need, Princess?" squeaked Petal. I was seeing a pattern here.

"Um, no need to call me princess."

The women turn to each anxiously and then curtseyed saying, "Sorry Your Highness."

"No, no, no." I get up from my bed. So much for getting to relax. "You can call me Imotenya."

"Mistress Imotenya?" asked Miracle.

"Just Imotenya."

"But that wouldn't be proper," scolded Hanna. She definitely was at the palace for a long time. I sigh, "I'm just Imotenya when we're alone okay?"

Hanna looked uncertain but Miracle and Petal seemed quite receptive to the change. "You may go now."

"But her majesty said we were to make sure at least one of us stayed with you at all times." For pity's sake!

"Well there are guards outside and I'll lock the balcony door." Providing it actually locks.

"Imotenya I don't think..."

"What if I'm ordering you leave?"

They looked at each other again before curtseying. "Yes, Mistress Imotenya," said Hanna. It was a start. "We'll go work on your outfits."

I nodded politely before they left, closing the door behind them.

Finally, I was alone. My eyes scan the room in disbelief, the cream walls and white wood furniture — demure and elegant. Still, it needed a personal touch. I checked around for my suitcase wondering if it was still in the car, but then I saw its worn out handle peeking from under the desk.

I opened it up on my bed, pulling out my necklace. I didn't want to put it in the drawer yet and so decided to put it on. I pulled out the scarf and lay it across one of the pillows. Maybe now it would smell like my old house for a while. Lastly, I took out an old cake-tin that held my letters. I wondered if mother and father kept the letters that I sent them. If when they felt alone or missed the sound of little feet around the halls, she would pull out those letters to let herself know that I was okay — that I was safe.

I took out each bundle from the tin. I'd tied the letters from Mama in pink thread, the letters from Baba in blue and the few ones from others in white. I took one from the white bundle. The handwriting was atrocious, but it had been familiar to me for some time.

It was from my cousin Best. I received the first one when I was eight years old.

To cousin Imotenya,

How are you? My mum says you won't remember me so she made me put in a photograph.

I looked at said photograph and saw a younger me in a frilly pink dress and tiara staring in awe at a huge cake in the shape of a '1'. A boy in a suit stood beside me and he looked as if he was going to jump head first into my cake. That must have been Best.

Mum says that you are living in Sapele. I've never been there but I hope to see you some time. Maybe you could come over. It must be really boring over there but I guess it's safe for you. In history, we talked about the law change. Our teacher said it's very bad to break tradition but I think some traditions have to be broken. I mean they used to kill twins in Calabar and that was bad.

I hope to hear from you soon. What class are you in? What do you do for fun in Sapele.? What's your favourite food?

I have to go now. Patience is crying because I won't let her write my letter. Maybe when she can actually write she can be sending you letters too. Bye.

From cousin Best.

I can't remember much of what I wrote back. I must have told him that I was homeschooled and liked to run and play tennis. I think I told him that my favourite meal at the time was noodles because he wrote back telling me that I should fry them.

The letters continued until a couple of years ago when he started preparing for his exams. After that, I never heard from him again. I thought I had lost the only friend I had outside of Sapele. The only person who reminded me of my life before.

I found the last letter that I received from him mixed with the letters from my father. So much for trying to be organised. The handwriting was so much better that I didn't have to turn it to the side to see some words when I first got it.

Dear Imotenya,

I can't believe it! You haven't changed a bit from your last photo but you still look very nice though. You do not know how lucky you are that you don't have to go to school. The BECEs are coming up and I feel so unprepared. Mum got me a tutor for maths and business. Those are my worst subjects. I am definitely dropping business next year. My father is away again. I wish he wouldn't go for so long. I really hope we get to meet sometime soon. I don't trust your pictures. I have to go, Mum's calling.

Write to you soon,
Best

He never replied to the letter I sent back to him. I never tried sending another letter. I just didn't see the point at the time, but the truth was I didn't want to seem too desperate. I couldn't. I was a princess which meant I had to show strength and dignity which I at least tried to do.

I put the letter back in its bundle and flopped back unto my bed. I wasn't going to sleep again, not if I wanted to sleep at night, so I got up and went to my balcony. It had gold railings in the pattern of a whale and vines were wrapped along them.

As if that wasn't enough, the view from the top was amazing. Below were the royal gardens which were in full bloom this time of year. I could see the patches of orchids and roses. Beyond the wall, I could get a glimpse of the city. I couldn't hear the traffic but I could imagine the flying taxis, the cries of bus conductors and the shouts of street vendors. The whole city was bright and vibrant even in the midst of death, yet there was still that stillness in the air. Suddenly, my maids came bursting in through the doors. I nearly jumped out of my skin when I saw their frazzled looks.

"Mistress, we're sorry to disturb you," gasped Hanna, already shuffling me to the vanity; Miracle, having free range of the wardrobe, pulled out a black dress while Petal took out a makeup palette. "But we have to get you ready."

"Ready? Ready for what?" I was surprised. I had just gotten back, what could be so important right now?

"Your uncle," breathed Miracle. "He's coming."

Chapter 5

I couldn't believe it. Sure, he would come to pay his respects, but on the exact day his brother died and the day his niece returned to the palace? I almost fell out of the chair. The man my parents wanted to protect me from was coming today. Then I remembered that I was the heir now. I was older and stronger now. I was the kingdom's new hope. I had nothing to be afraid of.

"Smile," said Petal with a blush sponge in her hand. I did as she powdered my cheeks.

I put on my new dress and looked in the mirror. Hanna insisted that I tie my hair up to make it look somewhat presentable. I looked ready.

"Thank you," I said to my maids. They looked extremely grateful as if for all the work that they did, no one ever thought of giving them any thanks at all. "You're welcome, princess," replied Hanna with a smile.

"Oh, my dear!" came a voice from the door. I turned to see that it was Mother clutching her heart. I couldn't tell if it was at the sight of me or the thought of my snake of an uncle coming to visit. "You look beautiful."

"Thank you, Mother," I said bowing a little. I would have kneeled if the dress wasn't so tight.

She came up to me quickly putting her hands on my shoulders just like David used to do. It wouldn't hurt to see him right now.

"Imotenya," she began. "Your uncle Lucky is coming from Lagos with his son. It would be rude to prevent him from seeing his own brother and he hasn't said anything about staying at the palace." That was a relief. "There will be guards around the room and I will be there myself to make sure that nothing funny goes on." I nodded before she took my face in her hands and looked me in the eyes. "Do not be afraid of him okay?" I had a feeling that she was talking to herself rather than to me, but I reassured her nonetheless.

She straightened herself up and gave me a quick inspection. "Shall we?"

"Lets."

I smiled in thanks at my maids who gave me encouraging looks. I think uncle dearest had a bit of a reputation.

I stepped outside and saw two guards standing outside my door. They bowed their heads in respect to us. I turned to see another guard coming towards us. I didn't know any of the guards at the palace, but this one seemed familiar. He came closer and I saw that it was David. It hadn't occurred to me before that I hadn't ever seen him in uniform. I guess it was part of helping me stay incognito but, still seeing him now, he looked more mature somehow.

He bowed to us and his eyes met mine for a second. "My queen, princess," he said before acknowledging the guards at my door. "Are you ready to go down?"

"Yes," Mama replied, her eyes steady and not betraying any uncertainty. Could I ever learn to do that?

We went back down the stairs, David following close

behind. I kept stealing discreet glances at him, but that wasn't possible so I recreated what I saw a few minutes ago. The way his shirt clung to his arms, the high collar drawing attention to his taunt neck, the confidence in his walk. That stirred something inside me. When had he gotten so desirable?

I shook my head. In only a couple of hours I had gone through several emotions: shock, grief, sadness, fear, whatever it was compelling me to turn around and look at my guard. In other words, I had to get control of myself.

We came to the ground floor and it looked like the maids had finished cleaning that area when a woman in a black skirt and blouse and exceptionally high heels came striding towards us. She was on the phone, but stopped completely and bowed before my mother.

"Your Majesty, I was just on the phone with His Highness's man and…" She saw me and the curious look on my face and her eyes bulged.

"Oh my. How are you, Your Highness?" She gasped taking me in. "I'm sorry but she's so beautiful."

"Um, thank you," I managed. I didn't need to turn around to know that David was laughing at me. I had never been good with compliments. Then she took my hands.

"I am so sorry about your father. I can't even begin to imagine how you are, but don't worry. If you have any trouble just come to me, Auntie Aisha, okay?"

"Okay." Just how old did she think I was?

"Aisha, what is happening with His Highness?" my mother said in a stern voice. This Aisha must have had a habit of drifting off topic.

"Oh yes, Your Majesty. Well, he and his son are arriving at the airport in a couple of minutes and a car has been arranged to collect them."

A few minutes? That meant that my uncle was probably already on the plane when he let us know that he was coming or mother knew and just wouldn't tell me.

"Well, we must be ready to meet him. Did his man say if they plan to stay at the palace?"

"No, my queen, he didn't but I can call to ask if you like…"

"No that won't be necessary. We'll deal with the matter when he arrives."

"All right, my queen," she chirped, but that didn't stop her from going back on her phone after a quick bow and then going on her way down the hall.

"And that was my secretary."

"Does it feel tiring?" I asked.

"Having people wait on you? I don't suppose so, but that doesn't mean life isn't busy."

"That's true." I thought of what it would be like if we had servants back in Sapele. We didn't even have a house-girl. Not that we couldn't afford it with funds from the palace. Judith told me a lot of stories of house-girls who beat the children and stole from the house and even one who began an affair with her mistress' husband. I guess we were saved from all that.

We went back to the sitting room which was now empty. I wondered where my aunties had gone. Mother went back to her chaise while David stood in the corner. Would he ever get to sit down?

I went back to my seat and just wrung my hands. My uncle and my cousin were arriving any minute now. I caught David's eye and then looked at my mother who was engrossed in a set of papers. I wished that we were alone so I could tell him all that was going on in my head about the situation at hand.

I made my way to a bookshelf that was close to where David was standing. As if on cue, he turned to me slightly and whispered: "Is everything all right, Your Highness?"

"You heard the attendant. My uncle is coming today."

My eyes scanned the books so as not to arouse suspicion from Mama.

"You have nothing to worry about. Specific instructions were given to keep an eye on him and his son."

I nodded. I could trust the palace guards. And if I couldn't, I could trust my mother. And if I couldn't trust her... I stopped. Why was I even considering that I couldn't trust her? I didn't know, but in the hopefully rare case that I couldn't trust her, I always had David. He'd stuck with me up till now.

"Thanks, and by the way, nice uniform."

He chuckled and whispered back, "Glad you like it, Your Highness."

"Imotenya," my mother called. Our moment was over so I picked a random book and went to sit back down.

"Yes Mother," I said, opening the book which, then looking at it, I found was a romance novel. How ironic. There was absolutely nothing romantic about the situation I was in.

Mother smoothed back my hair and rearranged my dress. Then she took my hand in hers and gave me a reassuring smile.

I didn't know how much I needed that because a few minutes later there was a knock on the door. We all straightened up as my mother said in her calmest voice, "Come in."

A steward came in and said, "Your Majesty, His Royal Highness and his son have arrived." Mother took a breath and stood up. "Send them in."

He nodded and went back out leading a tall dark man into the room. He had a full beard and walked with a cane. His eyes were intense and clouded, which I was sure were hiding something. He was wearing a black suit instead of the traditional agbada. I guess life in Lagos was pretty different compared to Beni.

His son followed behind him a little uncertain of himself. He, like his father, was wearing a suit with a navy-blue tie. His hair, like David's, was short but a little stood out on top. He had light-brown eyes that held none of his father's shiftiness. On the contrary, he seemed to be as curious about me as I was about him. Somehow, I thought he wasn't Best. Best, from his letters, sounded livelier than the boy standing in front of me.

They both bowed and Mother gave me a look as if to say 'They may bow to us now, but that doesn't mean they don't want the throne for themselves.'

"Your Majesty, my dear sister," said Uncle Lucky, taking Mother's hand in his own, looking so remorseful. "I can't tell you how sorry I am for what's happened."

"Thank you," Mama replied icily. "It was very kind of you to visit us in our distress."

"Not at all." My uncle was smiling now evidently taking pleasure in all of this. "I was coming to Beni anyway when I heard the news."

What a coincidence!

Mama turned to my cousin who quickly came over and knelt at her feet.

"Auntie." He said. He even sounded unsure of himself.

"Rise my boy," she said gently. He did and gave her a hug. Then he saw me and bowed.

"Cousin Imotenya," he greeted coming closer and I saw David stiffen a little. "It's so nice to finally meet you." He gave me a firm handshake, the only show of power I'd seen from him.

"Nice to meet you too," I said. I had no reason to be unkind to him. We had no quarrel. This was all between our parents, one of which was coming my way with open arms and a sinister looking smile.

"Teny!" he called out joyously, wrapping his arms around me.

"Hello Uncle," I muttered, praying to every single deity that I didn't stay in his embrace a moment longer than I had to.

He finally pulled back, but looked me over making my skin crawl.

"You're so big now," he said almost in thought as if he didn't expect me to live this long.

"I'm turning 16 next month." I don't know why I said that. Probably to show him that I was not as young as I seemed.

"Really, I thought you'd be older."

I smiled automatically. "You're shorter than I expected, Uncle." Both David and my cousin had trouble stifling their laughter while my uncle looked taken back.

"Sister Osoye and Ayela are here," interrupted my mother grabbing my uncle by the shoulder. "Would you like to see them?"

A pleased look came upon my uncle's face as he offered my mother the crook of his arm.

"Yes, I would." Then he nodded his head towards his son. "Keep the princess company and for the love of God don't slouch!"

My cousin managed to straighten himself up as he went to sit on the chaise. My mother gave David a 'keep her safe look' before leaving with my uncle. A silence ensued when I went back to pick up my book.

"What are you reading, Teny?" my cousin asked before quickly adding, "Do you mind if I call you Teny?"

Yes, I minded. I minded very much.

"It's just because you're so small, it suits you."

He had better watch his mouth. I clutched the book harder in my hand. For what it's worth, this day just got interesting.

Chapter 6

A few minutes later, a maid came in with a tray of drinks in her hand. I suppose they were meant to anticipate our needs. I thanked her as she put it down on the table between me and my cousin. I needed a drink if I was going to spend time with him.

"I'm sorry," I said, taking a sip of my Sprite. "I didn't get your name."

He looked at me over his glass and said, "Alexander. Cousin Alexander."

"Oh," I replied, taking another sip to avoid having to say another word too quickly.

"Sorry about your father," he said, not meeting my eyes. I couldn't ever see the throne going to him even under the old system. If he couldn't even look me in the eye, what hope did he have of being king?

"Thank you," I replied.

"I doubt you remember much of him though. Because you weren't here so much." I would have raised a single eyebrow if I could.

"And you do?"

He crossed his legs and leaned back a little in his chair.

"Well, not much of course; the last time I saw him was

two months ago in Lagos."

My heart ached. Two months ago, he hadn't even sent me a letter. He hadn't even had a desire to visit me.

"The king was very kind to me when I saw him," Alexander continued. "He didn't even look sick. He looked very strong. Who would have thought?"

It was too much. I got up abruptly and dusted imaginary dust from my dress. "I'm sorry," I said. "I just want to be alone for a minute."

"Are you all right?" asked Alexander worriedly. Or, at least, trying to sound worried.

"Yes, I'm fine," I rushed out the door nearly startling the guards. I turned back into the room and whispered to my guard, "David, you count as alone." I needed to let him know I didn't intend to go back in for a while.

He came out and started following me down the halls at a far enough distance that I didn't feel smothered and close enough so he could act if necessary. But now I didn't care if we were actually attacked, there was a lot going on inside me.

We came close to an alcove with a bench inside. I ran to it in quite an undignified manner, but at least David was the only one there and I was way past the point of impressing him if he hadn't forgotten my running around in tights days.

I collapsed onto the bench, taking in shallow breaths.

"Ria?" asked David with a hand on my shoulder. "Are you sure you're alright?"

"What do you think?" I said picking at the hem of my dress. It was shorter than the one I had one earlier, but with longer sleeves. An odd combination, but it worked.

I looked up at him trying to keep the wavering out of my

voice. "It's strange to think that the son of the most hated man in Xavia spent more time with my own father than I did," I said.

"I wouldn't say most hated," said David leaning back against the alcove wall. "He is up there with the people who made Ovaltine."

I coughed out a laugh and he smiled at me. How I wished I could bottle that smile and take it with me anywhere. I would never be miserable again.

"You're right," I said. "God knows what they were thinking."

"But seriously," said David, breaking all protocol by coming to sit right next to me. "He didn't say anything to make you upset, did he?"

I sighed, wringing my hands. "No, not really."

"Are you sure? Because if he did, I'm sure they'll be no problem for them flying back to Lagos."

"Can we hang them by their toes in the courtyard?"

He chuckled at that and then looked at me with an odd sort of admiration.

"The only thing I wish for you, Aria," he said softly. "Is that they never change you."

"Oh, there you are!"

We both jumped apart as my mother and my uncle came into view. David resumed his standing position and I clasped my hands nonchalantly in front of me. Why did I feel like I'd been caught somehow?

"I just needed some air, that's all, nothing serious," I said.

"Who could blame you, after what happened this morning and your journey here," said my uncle looking pitifully at me.

"I'm fine," I affirmed.

He nodded, but his gaze was on David who didn't even flinch. I admired his strength.

Mama came and put her arm around me as if I had just broken down into tears.

"The king will be passing," she whispered, holding me tighter. I really didn't want to leave my alcove, but soon enough we were walking back down the hall near the front door.

There he lay in his coffin surrounded by some stewards and his personal guards. He didn't look any different from when I saw him upstairs but his hair seemed combed back a bit. My aunties stood to the side and then came to embrace Mama. Uncle Lucky peered into the coffin with a sorry expression on his face and probably trying to make sure that his brother was actually dead. Cousin Alexander just lowered his head in reverence before the stewards closed the coffin and carried it out into the courtyard where he'd be brought to the chapel before the burial.

We all stood there in a sombre silence that was broken by Auntie Ayela's, "I think we all need a drink." There were murmurs of agreement as we made our way back to a slightly bigger living room with a television and plush red couches. The walls were aligned with masks and ornaments, mostly bronze. There was even a portrait of what looked like my great-great-grandfather.

With some bad luck, I ended up seated between my uncle and Alexander. Auntie Ayela had gotten another drink that I thought was vodka and she sat down beside Auntie Osoye who silently shook her head in disapproval. Mama sat in an armchair arranging a file of official looking papers. I wondered if that task would fall to me sometime soon.

"Imotenya, I forgot to say how beautiful you look," said Uncle Lucky suddenly.

"Oh." I was completely caught off guard, "Thank you, Uncle."

"You know the hard work begins tomorrow," he mulled, stirring his chardonnay.

"What do you mean 'hard work'?" I asked. Was his compliment just a way to butter me up for the incoming attack?

"Well, in your circumstances, all eyes will be on you in the coming days."

He turned to his son and saw that he was engrossed in a conversation with my aunties. Uncle looked at me and sighed. "Your mother," he began. "Has led a tough life."

Why was he telling me this?

"You do know that she had two miscarriages before she had you."

I nodded. Before she had me, there was another baby, a prince, who died in his sleep before I was born.

It was a commonly known fact that after she had me, she was told not to try and have another child or else she could damage her body. I always thought there was an underlying damage already. When I saw her on TV and in photos, she looked radiant of course, but there was something weak and tired about her.

"It was amazing how she fought against a long-standing tradition for her child. It showed a great amount of courage."

"Not misplaced I hope."

He didn't say anything, but put his fist under his chin and looked at me as if seeing for the first time.

"We shall see, Teny, we shall see."

Then he smiled and got up from the seat and made his way to my mother. Before I could process what he said Auntie Ayela plunked down in his place, her glass full (I wonder what she'd look like without a glass in her hand) and starting tittering on about her children who were studying in Ghana and another auntie of mine who lived in London and how she'd give me her number so she can send me things and a whole lot of other things that I could only nod at.

I glanced across the room to where David and my mother were in conversation; well, Mama seemed to be giving him a set of instructions.

Were they about my uncle and cousin? Was she still worried that we were under threat from them?

I wanted to get closer to hear what they were saying, but it felt rude leaving my auntie who was at this point clearly drunk that she ended up passing out quietly. I wonder how that was possible for her.

I got up slowly to Mama when David stepped back quickly to his corner of the room. I sat down beside her as she shuffled her sheets into a neat pile.

"Are you busy Mama?" I asked, still eyeing the pile. What were they about? She pushed them further across the table.

"No," she said a little too quickly, but then she caught me still looking at the papers. "I have to look over the plans for the burial."

"Already."

She sighed, staring at the portrait on the wall. I wonder if he reminded her of my father. "The king's heart was weak and we were told to prepare for the worst."

I wasn't told. My father mentioned nothing in his letters at all about having a weak heart. Even Alexander said he didn't look weak when he saw him two months ago. Or was that part of the 'Royals-Show-No-Weakness' deal or Alexander was just dumb. I surely believed it was the latter.

"Oh."

"It's nothing for you to worry about," she said, taking my hands in hers which didn't seem so small anymore. "Nothing to worry about, baby."

"I'm not a baby though," I said. So much for not feeling small. Mama laughed. The first I'd heard from her all day.

"It's going to be hard to not see you as the little thing that wouldn't stay in her crib."

I smiled at that thought. Ma Osa never usually brought up what I was like when I first arrived. Perhaps I could find out more by being around my immediate family. Other than how to put up with nonsense.

"Come," Mama said, getting up from her seat. "It's time for dinner."

Chapter 7

Dinner passed by, eventless, and soon all of us just wanted to go to our rooms for the night. We said our goodnights which ranged from hugs and pecks on the cheeks to unspoken death wishes.

David approached me while I was coming out of the dining room with an uneasy look on his face.

"Princess..." he began, but I took him by the wrist to a corner by the staircase.

"You called me 'princess'. Is something wrong?" I asked. He never called me 'princess'.

He bit down on the scar on his lip with his arms crossed against his chest. There was something wrong.

"The queen has asked..." he said eventually. "That you sleep in her room."

"What?" I gasped. Was I hearing correctly?

"She asked that..."

"I heard you before!"

David looked around to see that no one heard my little outburst but I didn't care. One of the perks of being in the palace was having my own bed in my own room.

"It's for security purposes now that you're back at the palace."

Mama must have thought that if anyone tried to come in the night to kill me, she could press herself between me and them.

"This is ridiculous," I said. She should move Uncle Lucky's bed to her room to make sure he doesn't get up to any mischief if she's so worried. "I'm going to speak to her."

"I wouldn't do that if I were you," he said, now holding onto my wrist. "She was very adamant about it."

I tried to pull my wrist out of his grip before turning around quickly to face him.

"Next time," I sighed resignedly, "You tell me about things like this as soon as you hear them." David took a more authoritative stance which I'd never seen before.

"I'm sorry Your Highness, but my orders don't come from you."

I would have stood there with an open mouth, but I didn't want to look stupid in front of him and my cousin Alexander just appeared in front of us with a glass in his hand.

"Excuse me," he said looking back and forth between me and David uneasily. "I didn't mean to interrupt anything."

"Oh, you didn't," I replied, plastering a smile on my face, but he didn't seem reassured. He kept looking at David as if he was some lion who had monstrously attacked a helpless lamb.

"Are you sure you're alright, cousin?"

"Yes, I am."

At this point, I just wanted to leave them both and get into my bed, wherever it was. "Well, have a good night," I said, already hurrying up the stairs not caring if David was following behind me. I turned around and he was. He didn't say a word as we approached my room. It was his own cup of tea.

I opened the door where Miracle and Petal were working on a dress and, funnily enough, my bed was gone. I had to appreciate that they didn't put in some new bed that I wasn't accustomed to.

They got up and curtseyed, but I didn't address them and stared at the empty space. The room felt much bigger now.

"Princess," said Miracle. "We thought you would like some things to take to the queen's room for the night."

She went to my wardrobe and pulled out three nightclothes, handing one to Petal and holding the other two up herself.

One was a red chiffon nightgown with a ruffled bodice. The other was a yellow silk nightdress with straps and the last one was a grey two-piece with short sleeves. I would have been comfortable with my usual vest and shorts so I picked the two-piece.

"Hanna will be in the queen's chambers in any minute," said Miracle in her chipper manner. "Is there anything else you'll need for now, Princess?"

"No, I'm fine for now."

She nodded helping Petal gather up their sewing. "Goodnight, highness," they said with a bow and left the room.

I took a look round my room like I did the first time which was rather stupid really. This room was still mine. It was only down the hall but I was really looking forward to sleeping in it tonight. Well, I suppose there'll be other nights. Hopefully, before I'm queen.

Queen. The future that for me was inevitable if I lived long enough. I hadn't been able to even comprehend that until today.

I took one last look where the bed had been and sighed before leaving the room. David had obviously been pacing because his face looked a little flushed.

"Got everything you need?" he asked with no hint of sarcasm which, with the amount of time I had spent there and what I had in my hands, would have been appropriate.

"Think so," I replied.

He nodded and then led the way towards the queen's chambers, no word said between us.

I began to feel really sorry about how I had reacted. He was just doing his job and perhaps it wouldn't be wise to have a go at my mother about such a trivial thing tonight. I held my nightclothes closer to my chest as we were at the queen's chambers. There were guards at her door.

Once inside, there was no argument. It was the most beautiful room I had ever seen. It was a light shade of lilac with blue accents. It had a small sitting room with mahogany chairs and a white chaise.

I heard voices coming from the other side. We walked towards the other door which was Mama's bedroom. It wasn't called the queen's bedroom for nothing. The vanity where Mama and Hanna were had three mirrors and her wardrobe had three doors and a few drawers. The bed had purple sheets as well with egg coloured pillows. On either side were cream coloured night stands and near the window was my bed as I first saw it. I hurried over to make sure that Ma Osa's scarf was still on top. It wasn't.

"Who carried the bed here?" I asked nobody in particular.

"Some stewards," said Mama getting up and coming towards me. Trust her to not actually know a name. "What is it my dear?"

I didn't answer and began rifling through the pillows and the sheets. It wasn't there. "Princess," gasped Hanna. "Is everything all right?"

No, it wasn't.

"There was a scarf here, on the pillow," I said, "Have you seen it?" Hanna shook her head.

"Maybe one of the girls took it down to laundry, I remember it looked very dirty."

Dirty? I knew it wasn't royal approved or palace standard issue but it wasn't infested. Just old. "What was it doing in my daughter's bed?" Mama asked, giving Hanna a stern look.

"I put it there," I said, not wanting Hanna to get the brunt of any of this. "Ma Osa gave it to me." Mama didn't say a word and I didn't know if that was a bad sign.

"Well," she sighed eventually. "I'm sure if it has been washed properly, you'll find it tomorrow."

"I'll make sure of it, your Majesty," said Hanna with a bow before giving me an almost grateful look.

"Your Majesty." David called out from behind us looking a bit apprehensive at the situation. "I'd like to make a few last-minute checks on the room if I may."

"Of course, Officer Soro," said Mama with no hint of disturbance at what happened a few seconds ago.

David bowed before inspecting the room. He checked the locks on the window, under our beds and even in the wardrobe. Did they really think a rebel was going to risk hiding in the queen's wardrobe? Was palace security that bad before?

"Everything seems to be in order ma'am," David said, taking a few glances at the room. "I've already checked the parlour."

Mama just nodded, pulling her robe closer to her chest. The A.C was coming on now it seemed. David bowed and wished us goodnight before leaving the bedroom. I followed slowly behind him, but he caught on and turned around.

"Forgive me?" I said stretching out my hand. It was the best I could do. If I spoke like I did to my immediate seniors, I would have to get down on my knees. Funny, tradition or any rules don't apply to you if you're high up enough.

David looked as if he didn't know what I was talking about. Trust him to try to keep the peace in any situation. Maybe that's why he'd been assigned as my guard. They must have seen my brashness early on.

"There's nothing to forgive, princess. Goodnight," he whispered with a smile, taking my hand and kissing it. It felt wrong. Not the kiss. It was so light and lovely. No, the whole situation of goodnights. In Sapele it would be "Try to stay in your bed, little dove" as he'd tug playfully on my hair. Here it was chaste kisses with the watchful eye of my mother at the corner.

"Goodnight," I said but I didn't want him to go yet. I wanted to let him know how sorry I was for being so pretentious and rude. I may have been a princess, but that was no excuse to talk to anyone as I did not to mention someone who had always been there for me.

He bowed again with a smile and left the queen's parlour.

Without David and Ma Osa's scarf, I was without everything from Sapele for the first time today and only then did the reality sink in. This was my new life.

Chapter 8

"Here, let me help you with that," said Hanna pulling the black dress from over my head. It was awkward. I never let anyone dress or undress me when I was younger not to talk of at fifteen.

Then she shuffled me into the bathroom. It was a replica of my own except for the colour scheme which was a misty shade of red. Next, she made me step into the bath. In front of me was a small cabinet. I tried to look for the vanilla scented soap Mama used. It smelled oddly calming on her.

I didn't know how long I was in there for and Hanna didn't mention anything about timing me. That was until there was a knock on the bathroom door.

"Is everything alright in there?" Mama called.

"Yes, Your Majesty," replied Hanna. I heard her shuffling towels on the other side of the shower curtain. "We'll be out in a minute."

I never told her that.

"I'm not finished yet," I whined while lathering another round of soap in my hands.

"You must, Highness," Hanna implored. "Too long in the bath and your skin will wrinkle." She said that in the tone one would use to say, "Smoking will lead to cancer."

I conceded. With one last rinse out of spite, I stepped out of the bath and where Hanna met me with a towel.

When we were in the bedroom. Mama was reading a book in bed as if she hadn't just interrupted my state of attempted relaxation. Hanna helped put on my night clothes and even tied my hair upwards for sleeping while muttering about needing to do something with my hair first thing tomorrow.

"Anything else you need, highness?" Hanna asked as she made an opening in the covers to let me slip into.

"No, I don't think so," I said climbing into my bed. She bowed with a smile. "Your Majesty, highness."

She smiled again and went out of the bedroom and I heard the door to the suite close.

I turned to my mother's bed and saw that she was already asleep. I looked closer and saw faint streaks under her eyes. She had cried herself to sleep without saying goodnight.

I really felt alone.

I watched her chest rise and fall slowly, her book slid down to her stomach. I muttered a silent goodnight, turned off my lamp and went to sleep.

I woke up fifteen minutes later.

I felt a little disoriented when I didn't feel a small foot kicking my shins or a warm stomach behind me. Having your own bed wasn't all it was cracked up to be. For starters it made even Xavian summers feel cold. Secondly, it was kind of lonely. Mama was sound asleep, still breathing gently. I looked around her room and it didn't feel that much safer than my room.

How long would it be like this? And just like Uncle Lucky said, the hard work would start tomorrow and every day after that. I had studied for this all my life but did I really want it? To create history, to be a princess and eventually become queen?

The truth was I didn't. My father wasn't even around to show me the ropes. Sure, I had Mama, but being the wife of a king and being queen were two very different things. Then there were the chiefs. Would they accept and support me when some of their own funded and planned attacks on the monarchy?

It was all too much. At that point, I didn't care if a rebel came right then and shot me. Why would I? Then Uncle Lucky or whoever could take the throne and let me rest in peace. I felt hot tears stream down my face. I couldn't do this.

Before I realised it, I had thrown back the covers and ran out of the bedroom and into the parlour. I pulled the door open startling the guards but I ignored them even as they called out for me to stop.

I dashed down the stairs, stumbling over a few. My eyes were blurry with unshed tears and that didn't help. I could hear the shouts of guards when all I wanted was to escape, to get out to...

"Ah!" I crashed onto the floor using my arms to try and catch myself. Apparently, this side of the palace didn't have carpets. My elbows stung immediately. I felt for my legs, but they were raised because they were on something. On someone.

"Your Highness?" yelled a guard from the end of the corridor. Oh no. It was bad enough if the guards saw me cry, it'd be worse if they caught me sprawled on the floor on top of someone.

"Do you mind?" the 'someone' grunted trying to wiggle

out from under me. I saw that we were laying in front of a door. My chance to save face.

I hauled myself up and pulled on my crash victim's hand, opened the door and shoved them in then followed them just before I caught a glimpse of the guard's uniform. The room was dark, as I peered out to make sure that the guards had gone.

"What are you doing?" said my room buddy.

"Shush!" I hissed still watching the guards.

"I didn't see her," said one.

"Are you sure she came down here?" asked another. "Yes, she did."

"Should we ask His Highness?"

"You don't suppose he's taken her in do you?"

"No, he wouldn't dare."

The lights came on in the room. "What are you doing?"

I had forgotten for a moment that someone else was here with me. I closed the door as quietly as I could before turning to my roommate.

I held back a gasp. It was a young boy with curly hair who couldn't be that much older than me. His hand was on the switch with his other hand on his hip and a perplexed look on his face.

I opened my mouth but no words came out. Instead I broke down again, collapsing on the floor.

Great. Just my luck. This boy, whoever he was, was having a pretty good show. The future ruler of Xavia crying her eyes out on the floor. Yes, this was a good show indeed.

"Uhm? Are you all right?" asked the boy crouching down to my level. I didn't know why but I was mad. Mad at him for seeing me like this. Mad at myself for being so weak.

"Who are you?" I snarled. The boy looked a bit taken back. "Who are you?" I said a little louder.

"I'm a servant" said he and I thought how stupid I was. If he wasn't my uncle, cousin or my mother, he had to be a servant. "For His Highness."

I blinked. "Your uncle," he reiterated.

"Yes, I know who he is," I snapped.

He seemed to ignore my remark as he got up and turned to look at our surroundings. "I just wanted to see if he needed anything, before he went to sleep."

I nodded as I calmed down a bit but still didn't want to get up. He turned back to me and smiled.

"Nice room," he said cheerfully, his hands in pockets. It was kind of unnerving how calm he was even after being collapsed on and dragging him into a room on his first night. "I know why you were so eager to drag me inside, Your Highness."

I fixed him with a hard glare. "You know nothing about me." He shrugged. "I'm not sure anyone does."

He looked at the door, then at me as if I was going to pounce on him if he made a run for it. In the state I was in, I could have.

"Well," he said, finally walking towards the door. "If the threat has passed, I better be going." Before he even touched the doorknob, he turned back to me, bent down and bowed. "Goodnight Your Highness." Then with one last smile he was gone.

I remained there for a full five minutes still trying to catch my breath.

Another five minutes passed before the guards, which thank the Lord, including David, came to escort me to my room. It was all a bit much really, especially after I kept telling them that I just needed a bit of air and that was fine. They said that the queen was worried sick about me. I noticed the way they said 'the queen' and not my 'mother' as if at that I'd fall to my knees in apology. Well I didn't. I went back into bed with a sympathetic look from David and a breath-squeezing hug from Mama — it was a miracle I had enough breath to climb into my bed. At last, I fell asleep not thinking about my uncle, my mother, my father or being queen or any of that.

No, I thought of how I didn't catch the servant's name.

Chapter 9

I was roused by Miracle at around seven in the morning. It wasn't earlier than I was used to, but that didn't mean I was ready to get out of bed especially after last night.

After an assisted shower I was put in another in a black day-dress. Hanna and Petal came in a few minutes later to execute justice on my unruly hair. Black tufts fell down around me in quick succession that I was starting to get worried that my mother's idea of neat hair was cut down to the skin. Thankfully, when it was over, I still had hair on my head, but now it only touched below my collarbone. It was a weird feel.

"There," said Hanna putting down her scissors and smiling at me through the mirror. I looked at myself and felt odd all of a sudden. More grow-up. As if a pretty dress and a new hairstyle made me seem older. In a way I was, especially with the amount of makeup Miracle was putting on my face, probably to hide the circles under my eyes.

"Today's a special day, Princess," Hanna said cheerfully. "'You're meeting the chiefs today."

"The chiefs?" I asked. "Today?" Well, that explained the generosity of makeup.

"They'd want to meet the princess after her safe return."

I'm sure they would. I was feeling slightly nervous. Some

of the remaining chiefs who weren't outright rebels still didn't seem so sure about me taking the throne at least not yet.

There was a knock on the door and Petal went over to open it.

"Good morning, I hope I haven't woken her Highness."

It was David. He came into view with a calm look but he broke into a smile when he saw my hair.

"Good morning, Princess," he said looking at me in a way that made my cheeks heat up .

"Good morning Officer," I replied. We had company so we had to be formal.

"The queen has asked that I escort you to breakfast on the terrace."

"Oh." Sounded fancy for breakfast.

I got up out of my vanity chair and then turned to my maids. "Thank you," I said. They all smiled and curtseyed before David and I left the room.

He nodded to the guards outside my door as we walked down the corridor in a somewhat comfortable silence.

"How was your night?" David said finally.

"You mean apart from giving my mother a heart attack, getting chased by the guards and being found in a heap in some room," I said. "Quite uneventful."

He chuckled, placing a hand on the small of my back to lead me to where the terrace was supposed to be.

"What about you?" I asked.

"Apart from finding a runaway princess, quite uneventful." I laughed at that, but before I could retort a siren blazed.

It was eons since I heard it last, but I knew all too well

what it meant. Rebels.

In the flash of an eye, I saw my mother and aunties emerge running from a corner.

"Your Majesty, this way," David called out, a steely resolve on his face as we ran back down the corridor. We stopped at a painting of a sunset opposite a parlour. David pressed his hand against the bottom of the frame. Suddenly, the painting was pushed back revealing a staircase leading downwards. I certainly didn't remember that.

My mother and aunties went down immediately their footsteps receding quickly.

"Go," said David pushing me slightly. "Just go down and stay there until the all clear is given."

"What about you?"

"Go now!" he said pushing the painting back into place, leaving me in the dark.

"Imotenya?" Mama called, her worried face coming into view. "Come on."

I hurried down, profusely cursing the heels my maids made me wear. Honestly, who was going to care how tall I was if I was dead?

We ran down the stairs until we reached a room with concrete walls. It was as big as my father's bedroom with crates and coolers stacked to the side. A first aid box hung on a rack next to a sink with a cabinet. Along the wall were a few beds. On a nightstand in the corner was a radio. All of a sudden, my mother took me in her arms in a hug that was tighter than yesterday.

"Oh, my girl," she sighed in relief. "Are you all right?"

"Yes, Mama, I'm fine."

"To think, an attack this early in the morning; it's

ridiculous."

I turned to see my uncle and cousin standing towards the end of the room, directly opposite from my aunties.

"A day after the king's death," sniffed Auntie Osoye taking a drink of water. "These wyo people." My mother gulped suddenly, something I couldn't decipher coming over her. I brought her over to one of the beds and helped her sit down and knelt at her feet. I didn't ask her if she was all right because that was of course a stupid question. She had just lost her husband and now some terrorists were coming for her child. And she had to stay strong in all of this. No room for any show of weakness.

Out of the corner of my eye I glimpsed my uncle coming towards us.

"Eniola?" He said to my mother, placing a hand softly on her shoulder; the only decent gesture I've seen from him so far. "It will be over soon, it always was."

Mama nodded softly and smiled thankfully up at him, but that look cracked when we heard a distant crash. Auntie Ayela gripped the sink, Alexander flattened against the wall and even Auntie Osoye looked a bit apprehensive.

I thought of David. He said he'd been involved with the rebels when he was last here but he never went into details. To be honest, it was something we never talked about in Sapele. Sure there was the occasional newspaper or news segment, but I was somehow kept from any real information even in the letters I got. I wondered how he was if he was staring down a rebel right this second or...

No. The other possibility was too horrible to consider. I didn't even want to consider it. It would be like losing a whole part of myself. No, David Soro had to live.

We stayed there for almost half an hour until a guard came to announce to us that the threat had passed. Mama, although she tried not to show it, looked the most relieved. As we trekked back up the stairs, my thoughts were racing about what had happened. How far had they gotten this time? Not to sound morose, but how close was I to certain death?

"Teny? Are you okay?" I turned to Alexander, who walked closely alongside me. "Yes," I said. "Just the shock of it all but it's wearing out."

"Well, it was bound to happen sooner or later now that you're here." As if I didn't know that already.

When we got up, we saw that the hall as a whole was unscathed. The guard told us that it had mainly been the courtyard that was breached.

"Just a few knockouts thrown in," said the guard.

"Knockouts?" asked Alexander. "That is what they call an assassination attempt?"

"I don't think they were going to try to cause harm," said my uncle a little too nonchalantly. "So is it safe to go about our business now?" asked Auntie Osoye impatiently.

"Yes," replied the guard turning to Mama. "There is a clean-up on the ground floor but other than that, there's no cause to worry, your Majesty."

Mama nodded and motioned him to get to his duties. My aunties, uncle and cousin excused themselves after the ordeal and just as I thought it would just be me and Mama, Aisha came running down the hall.

"Your Majesty, Highness," she called out before stooping into a bow. "Thank goodness you're both all right. How frightening it must have been for you my dear…"

"Aisha what is it?" Mama cut in.

"Oh," gasped Aisha as if she had forgotten that she actually had something useful to say. "Yes, I need to inform you that the chiefs have arrived."

"Already?"

"Yes, madam."

A flash of uncertainty crossed Mama's eyes before she replied, "Then we will meet them at once."

She turned on her heel back down the hall, while I and Aisha followed along, me feeling less than thrilled to have been through an attack on the palace, having to meet a bunch of self-important chiefs the day after my father's death, listening to the endless chatter of my mother's secretary and all on an empty stomach.

Chapter 10

The guard wasn't joking about a clean-up being done on the ground floor. There was dirt on the windows, a few ornaments were broken on the floor. I saw David in a doorway talking to another guard. Thank God he was all right. He looked my way and mouthed an 'Are you all right?' I smiled and gave him a thumbs up. He then gave me a look meaning we would talk later and followed behind us.

I turned to see that Mama and Aisha had already left the building. I ran in the midst of the bowing servants and guards. I wonder how they felt with all the attacks. I know the guards would spend most of the time trying to stop the perpetrators in their tracks but what about the

servants? Did they have safe rooms? And more importantly what about my maids. I was starting to worry about them even though the damage done was only superficial.

"Imotenya?" Mama called a little way off. I picked up the pace, approaching the courtyard that was also in a state. I felt sorry for those in charge of cleaning it up.

Eventually, we entered the administrative building. It's red and gold colour scheme was similar to that of the living quarters, but photographs and plaques of historical significance lined the walls instead of ornaments. I glanced at the few that had carvings of what seemed like my past kings slaying animals or holding feasts. We then came to a chamber with a fountain in the centre. Water spurred from the top then cascaded into a hole in the marble floor. Sitting on a bench under one of the coconut trees sat the chiefs. I had recognized most of them from the TV and newspapers, all from the seventeen remaining states of Xavia.

There used to be thirty six a long time ago, but the northern states broke away and formed their own country. Another three tried to break away sixteen years ago when I was announced heir. Even the ones sitting in front of us now weren't all so clear-cut on their alliances; nevertheless, they rose up then bowed as soon as they saw us. One of them, Chief Oluwade from Kogi I think, stepped towards my mother and bowed again.

"Your Majesty, we are all sorry for the loss of the king," he said and others murmured in agreement. They all sounded as if they truly meant it, which I'm sure they did. We were all in a very uncertain time now.

"Thank you," Mama replied with a serene look on her face. The mask that showed no sign of crumbling.

"We heard that there was an attack on the palace," said Chief Agoto of Benue. "We all feared for your safety majesty." The chiefs nodded. "And the safety of the princess." There were fewer responses meaning they were quite divided on that one.

"Well as you can see, we are perfectly fine," said Mama serenely and walked in front of the chiefs each greeting her in turn. They did the same to me and I responded with a polite nod of the head. Whether dealing with chief or civilian, a nod and smile seemed to always go a long way.

Suddenly, Chief Agoto began to step closer towards Mama.

"Your Majesty," he whispered. "Let us not beat about the bush. You must know what we are here to discuss." The queen nodded solemnly.

"In private," he added. I hesitantly looked around. It was just Mama, me, David, the chiefs and some surrounding guards. Then I understood. This meeting wouldn't include me.

Mama gave me a smile and told me that I could go back for breakfast with David, and that the meeting wasn't any of my concern. I had a feeling that the whole subject was me. She then led the chiefs to a door leading to some sort of conference room. As soon as the last man was inside the guard slammed it shut, as if putting a strong emphasis on the confidentiality of the meeting.

"Let's go," said David, placing a hand on the small of my back as we left the room.

"Well they seemed friendly," I said thinking about my introduction if one could even call it that. I thought that the chiefs would be introduced to me and not the other way round. Perhaps, they thought as heir apparent, I should be fairly up to date on current affairs.

"They have no choice," David replied, straightening his holster. "They can't make a bad representation of their states."

"Representation?"

"Yes, didn't you notice that very few of the chiefs were there. Most of them were representatives, sons and ambassadors." Some of the men were unrecognisable and quite young for chiefs.

"Anyway, I think from what I saw, you held yourself quite

well."

"You think so?" I asked.

"I really do."

A light feeling came on me as I looked at the sure look on his face. If David thought I did well, then I had no care. At least until I saw my uncle coming up the steps of the building. He had no business here. He was just a guest.

"Imotenya, my dear," he called out with open arms. After yesterday, I was in no hurry to get back into them again.

"Uncle," I said with an attempt at enthusiasm. "What a pleasant surprise."

"I'm glad to see that you're up and about. Most girls would have to be confined for their own good, but you are being very strong my dear."

I clenched and unclenched my fists. "I would have to be. These are dangerous times we are living in."

I made no effort to hide the accusations, but he came closer to me with a disturbing ease. "Those uzamas," he sniffed. "Are just graduated trouble-makers. Look, all they did today was make a mess."

"Begging your pardon, Your Highness," said David coming up from behind me and staring uncle dead in the eye. "But what do you presume would have happened if they reached inside the palace." Uncle Lucky gave a grim smile, but just ignored David and leaned towards me.

"In all truth, my dear, most of the time it's not those outside we need to worry about. A man's enemies are those in his own household."

In his own household? Uncle gave a smile and a bow of the head.

"Your cousin is in the library, but maybe he'll be a better

companion for you today, but I must go."

He walked in the direction in which we had come from like he was on a mission. What did he mean by what he had just said? If he was trying to divert any suspicion of himself, he was making a huge mistake. He was family and he was in my household.

I felt a tap on my shoulder and turned slightly to see David staring worriedly at me.

"Hey," he said, "Are you all right?"

"Uhm, yes, just hungry I suppose."

His expression hardened and his hand shifted to his holster. "I should never have let that man near you."

I scoffed, "Sticks and stones can break my bones, but words can never hurt me, David. And, besides, he was harmless enough."

"Let's hope that he stays harmless."

I agreed, but still couldn't forget what uncle had told me. I needed something to take my mind off it.

"David, are you busy?"

My guard smirked. "I'm only as busy as you are, highness. hy do you ask?"

"Do you want to have breakfast with me?"

He looked a little uncertain and I almost couldn't understand why. In Sapele, David always sat with us at every meal, like he was part of the family, I didn't think it would change here.

"I'm not sure your aunties would like me there."

"Who says it has to be on the terrace or in the dining room," I said. "We could have a tray brought up to my room, I'm sure I'm allowed to eat in there."

"Aria," he sighed. "That wouldn't be proper."

"What wouldn't be proper about it. You're my guard, what wouldn't be proper was if you never went into my room, like what if there was a bomb in there?"

"Aria, that would be most unlikely with the amount of rummaging that your maids do." I crossed my arms.

"Well, at least they're doing their jobs."

David groaned as I nodded at a few grounds men, who had stopped to bow.

"Please," I begged with a mock sullen look. "The last person you say no to is a princess, not to talk of a princess in mourning." I sniffed for added effect.

"All right," David conceded. "We'll have breakfast." I could have leapt for joy. A meal with just David and me would undoubtedly be ten times better than yesterday's lunch and dinner. The only thing that would have made it better was if Judith and Winter were here, but I tried not to think about that. Emphasis on the tried.

Breakfast turned out as I expected: bliss. Hanna had been in my room when we got there and I had told her to get us a breakfast tray. She seemed surprised when I said that David would be dining with me and would have rather stayed with us and got another girl to get the tray. She came back with a platter fit for a king, literally. There were slices of white bread and creamy margarine, akara and akamu with slices of grapefruit, mangoes and pawpaw on the side.

We even got hot chocolate to go with our meal. I dipped a slice of bread in my cup, careful to not let any chunks fall inside while David, who was sitting at my desk, gently placed his akara in his slice of bread. Funny, I was the princess and yet he was the one with the better table manners.

"This is nice," I mumbled contentedly while taking a sip of my chocolate.

"Nothing less should be expected in the palace," David replied, wiping crumbs from around his mouth. He missed a spot on his bottom lip. "Even for the guards. They're always expected to fatten up like pigs for the slaughter."

I couldn't ignore it any longer. I picked up a serviette and went up to him.

"'Like pigs' is right," I said. "You obviously don't know how to eat."

I dabbed at his lip lingering a little longer than necessary. I never realised how plump they were from all the biting. So full and beautiful. He stared at me with a hard to read expression. Was he angry with me? Did I cross a line? I pulled back, failing to meet his eyes.

"There, all better," I muttered, shuffling back to my place on the bed after quickly grabbing a piece of grapefruit. I shoved it in my mouth to avoid saying anything that would make this situation more awkward than it was while David took a sip of hot chocolate. I didn't even tell him that he was drinking mine.

After a few minutes of silence, there was a knock on the door.

"Come in," I called. It was one of the guards that was with us in Sapele. Officer Avril. After a brief greeting, he asked to speak to David. He got up to make his way towards him. They spoke in hushed tones which I really picked up on. Not that I even cared about what they were saying. No, at that moment, all I could do was glance at my cup. The place where David had drunk from. I picked up the cup and took a drink. It was cooler now but the rim was still warm from his lips.

The door closed and my guard came back and sat down.

"Is everything all right?" I asked, putting the cup down as confidently as possible. Now it was David's turn to eye the offending cup.

"He was just updating me on the new security measures being put in place."

"Oh, what are they?"

"Nothing for you to be concerned about though."

"Right, because my safety is none of my concern." He just smiled picking up another slice of mango.

"If I'm correct," he said, drawing the mango across his lips. "You'll be too busy to even notice where you are."

I wrinkled my nose at that. So far that was the only thing I was certain of. That I would be busy. "Well, that means you will be busy too."

"I have to agree to that."

I giggled. It wouldn't be so bad if David was with me, no it wouldn't be so bad at all.

"Do you think the meeting's over?" I asked, wiping my hands. "How long do they usually take?" David shrugged and sat back down. "It depends on what they're discussing and since it deals with the entire future of the kingdom, I suppose it'll take some time."

I thought about that. The monarch usually held supreme rule with a handful of advisors but the interests of the chiefs had always been considered or else uprisings could take place. My family, the Accras, fifty years ago had overthrown King Absalom Korade. I only wished that it wouldn't come round on us too soon. I didn't even want to consider that, not with the rebels already causing problems.

"Well, ,I'm done and have no clue what to do today."

"You could go find Aisha," David suggested. "You two could have a long monologue." My lips spread into a smile. "Sorry conversation." We both laughed at that.

After a brief talk, I decided that I wanted to write a letter to Winter and Judith. David was leaving, but assured me that there were others on patrol and that he'd still be around the hall. "Thank you for a wonderful morning, Highness," he said, backing towards the door with a salute. "You're very welcome Officer," I replied with a deep curtsey. David laughed before leaving with a final disarming smile. I smiled too. I couldn't help but feel so much lighter and comfortable whenever I was around David. It was even the same in Sapele, whenever Winter and Judith were at school and Ma Osa was running the shop, it was like we were in the same boat, both of us being away from home for the first time. We clung to each other then and we'd remained close ever since.

I took out a refill pad and sat down at my desk to write my letter:

To Winter and Judith,

How are you all? I hope you are well. The palace is nice. More than nice. There are so many pretty things. The food here is wonderful as well, almost as good as your mother's!

My mother is also well as she could be under the circumstances. I met my mother's sisters yesterday as well. They were interesting to say the least. His Highness, uncle Lucky and his son came to visit yesterday. They were as they say 'on their way to Benin' for what, I cannot say. I think you'd like his son Alexander though, Judith. He's cooped in the library right now.

How our plans changed so quickly this summer. We were meant to fry fish and go swimming. Not think about burying a family member because my family is your family too. Remember that. Thank your mummy and daddy for me, for everything. I miss you so much and it's only been a day. Write back soon and tell me everything. David sends his regards and probably would appreciate a letter as well. I could hand it to him if you like.

Hope to hear from you soon, Your adopted sister,

Aria.

P.S. Winter, the palace has a staircase but I've yet to slide down it yet!

Before I could even put my pen down, I heard a bang and a range of screams. All of a sudden, my door was flung open by Officer Avril.

"Princess!" He panted. "Are you all right?"

"Yes," I said, getting up quickly. "What was that sound?"

"Some of the guards are downstairs as we speak, Highness."

Another guard came running with Hanna, Miracle, and Petal by his side.

"Highness, I think's best that your maids stay with you until this is all sorted out," he said as Hanna took my hand to usher me inside along with Miracle.

"But what is going on?" I whined holding on to the door frame. Everyone seemed to want to protect me but were doing a really bad job of it. "What happened?"

"It was so loud," whimpered Petal wringing her hands. "Loud? What was that?"

"Stop fidgeting girl," snapped Hanna as we all went inside. Miracle pulled out my chair and tried to get me to sit down, but I wouldn't until I knew what in God's name was going on here.

I grabbed Petal by the wrist and she flinched. "Please tell me." She heaved in terror with tears glistening in her eyes.

"A bomb, Princess," she whispered. "It was a bomb." Then she collapsed.

Chapter 11

"Put her on my bed," I said urgently.

"Certainly not," gasped Hanna. "It would not be proper."

"Now!" I yelled.

Miracle slung Petal's arm over her shoulder and dragged her onto my bed. I found a white cloth and ran water over it in the bathroom. I came back and gave the cloth to Miracle. She placed it on her forehead and held her hand.

"Has this happened before?" I asked Hanna who stood at the side watching carefully. She looked quite hesitant in answering but sighed and said, "Not in a very long time."

I began to think back to the last few minutes. A bomb had gone off. Nobody had said where, but it seemed to have been outside the palace. And only a couple hours ago, there was an attack on the palace and the chiefs had arrived and my uncle was seen going into the administrative building.

The administrative building. The meeting with the chiefs. Mama. I started feeling sick all of a sudden. I had already lost one parent only yesterday. I couldn't lose her too.

Petal began to stir and open her eyes. She looked a little uneasy but when she saw me, her eyes filled with terror.

"I'm so sorry, highness," trying to get up but I shook my head.

"No," I said, "You're all right, lie down." But she was adamant and so we put her onto my chaise. There was still a jug of water from breakfast. I poured a glass for Petal which she took timid sips from.

I went over to Hanna who was rearranging my bed. She really was immersed in her work.

"You said this happened before," I said holding onto the side of the bed. She didn't say anything. I sat on the bed to make her stop her task. Eventually she sighed and said, "Petal used to live with her family in Gombe before she came to the palace. One day she was went to work as a house-girl for some woman while her mother and little brothers were at home. That was the day rebels attacked."

"Rebels?" I asked. I had heard that they had been involved in minor skirmishes in the past especially up north.

"Yes, they did a bombing campaign in that area. Petal's house was destroyed with all her family. The poor girl was in shock for weeks. An old friend arranged for her to work at the palace but, from what I heard, she has never been the same since."

I was shocked. It was beyond awful. No wonder she fainted. She had lost her entire family in one explosion, goodness knows what memories could have been brought back from today's. "But Your Highness," Hanna continued, fiddling with her apron. "I'd like to say that Petal is a very hard worker and loves her job here. I hope what happened won't make you change your mind about her post here."

I was shocked at that. If that happened to me and I wasn't the princess, I would have behaved just as she did or probably worse.

"I don't see why it should change anything," I said,

nodding at Petal on my chaise. "She's a really good girl."

Hanna smiled an almost melancholy smile. "That's very kind of you, Highness."

Before I could say another word, my door was opened by David who was the picture of concern.

"Sorry, Your Highness," he said. "Are you all right?"

"Yes," I gasped at the sudden interruption. "I heard about the bomb." "Yes," he sighed. "I'm sorry, but…

He paused and then took me by the wrist to the corner of the room. "Aria, I'm so sorry."

"What happened David? Please," Someone died. It had to be. He placed his hands on my shoulders and bit his lip again.

"I don't know how to tell you this," he began, "But His Highness is injured," I had heard incorrectly. I must have. My uncle, injured?

"What about Mama, David. What about Mama?" "The queen is fine and so are the chiefs."

I was beyond relieved. But then I thought about Alexander. Did he know? "I need to go see Alexander," I resolved. "I need to see him now."

"No Ria," said David shaking his head. "You can't, not yet. Your mother wishes to see you immediately."

"Now?"

"Yes now."

I couldn't believe what was happening. First my father, now my uncle. First the king, now the heir presumptive. First the queen's husband, now her brother-in-law. I should have felt a certain joy, but all I felt was empty and I couldn't imagine what Mama was feeling.

And I really had to see her. I had to support my family.

Hanna came up to say that they were taking Petal back to her room. David advised her that if need be, Petal should be taken to the medical bay and that it wouldn't be too full even with casualties. She thanked him and they picked Petal back up again and left the room.

David and I went back to my mother's room which was now surrounded by a plethora of guards. When I went in I saw my mother and Aisha sitting in the parlour. Aisha was the only one who acknowledged me. Mama and Alexander were just stooped over their cups of brandy, still as statues. I caught a glimpse of tears at the corner of Alexander's eyes, which he quickly dried away as soon as he saw me. His father may have been a rival for the throne, but he was still his father. I knew what it was like to lose a father. I wouldn't wish it on my worst enemy.

To hell with propriety, I strode up towards him and knelt at his feet, then took his hand. "I'm so sorry," I said. "Truly I am."

He didn't say anything. How could he?

Mama put her hand on my shoulder ushering me to rise and take a seat next to her. She didn't ask how I was. She knew better.

"Mama, will Uncle be alright?" I asked.

She still didn't look at me but just continued to stare at her cup. "Why today?" she sighed. "Why now?"

I didn't have an answer for that. I, against all sense and better judgement, hoped that uncle would be all right.

I heard static noise and turned to see David, fiddling with a radio. He picked it up from his belt and listened intently to what was being said. After a few seconds, he said "Alright," and put it back on his belt.

"Your Majesty," he said. "They've captured a man suspected of being a bomber." That got Mama's attention. Her head snapped up and finally put down her cup. "Where is he?" she asked in a monotonous voice.

"He's being taken to the prison for questioning."

She nodded and got up from her chaise, completely ignoring me. She whispered in David's ear with a solemn look, while he nodded obediently.

Did they even care that I was still there? My uncle had been attacked at what may have been meant for me or Mama. Was that what this all was about?

They eventually stepped out of the door and said things to the guards "...stay here?"

"...escort the Queen, I'll stay with the princess."

The last voice was David's. He backed into the room with two other guards as I heard the receding footsteps of my mother and her own entourage of guards.

"My auntie's," I gasped getting up. In all this, I had forgotten that there were other guests at the palace. "Where are they?"

"They are safe, Princess," said David ushering me to sit down but my body refused.

I couldn't believe it. I wouldn't believe it. Two days ago, I was a normal girl, living a normal life not a princess, whose father just died and whose home was just bombed. It couldn't be true.

I pushed myself past David and ran to the bathroom. I pressed myself against the toilet and hurled.

Aisha came and pulled what was left of my hair back.

"You're okay," she cooed, patting my back as I threw up again. "It's going to be alright." She continued this mantra until I felt a hand on my shoulder and a wet towel on my head.

"Princess, breath," a maternal voice whispered into my ear. I turned slightly to see that it was not my mother. It was Hanna with Miracle standing a little way off, looking anxious.

I wondered how it would have seemed that the kingdom's heir turned out to be a complete invalid. It wasn't long until a strong pair of arms came and carried me out after I was cleaned.

I was laid down on my mother's bed, hair being swept away from my eyes.

"Get the doctor."

It was the last thing I heard. The last thing I wanted to hear as I pulled my pillow over my head to snuff out the light.

Chapter 12

A couple of hours later, I was sitting upright in my bed with the palace doctor asking me a series of questions which for some reason seemed to increase in ridiculousness.

"Are you taking your vitamins?"

"Did you drink water from a well?"

"Are you pregnant?"

I could have laughed at the last one. The only men I had any contact with recently were David and Koda. The latter was very rarely around and the former, well, when it came to David, I just couldn't help those thoughts coming into my head. Though I knew he was far from capable of doing such a thing, the very thought caused a rising heat between my legs.

The doctor took my temperature and ran some tests, then finally announced that I was going through shock. I noticed how a simple word coming out of the mouth of a doctor could seem like a death sentence. Or worse. That bomb could have ended any of us if we were there at the wrong time but shock… When were we ever cured of a state of emotion?

"Well princess," said the doctor. "All I can advise you is to rest."

I barely heard Aisha mutter something about spending money on an education but only being able to prescribe rest.

For some reason I agreed with her. It would take a whole lot more than just rest to get me out of this state.

The doctor eventually left with Aisha to get the queen. Hanna sat beside my bed stroking my hair while Miracle made sure I was properly covered. Seeing them work without Petal felt wrong. I had only known her for one day and yet, I missed her quiet air like a feather on your cheek, that you don't realise was there until it's gone.

David watched me anxiously from the other side of the bed and I think that's what scared me the most. David was trained to be prepared in any situation. I was starting to think that he wasn't prepared for an heir in shock. And yet he stood there watching me intently.

"I'm fine," I kept muttering but it was no use. Hanna and Miracle continued to fuss and pander while David still watched me.

"Can I get something to eat?" I implored even though there still was something other than bile in my stomach.

Hanna squeezed her face. "Are you sure Princess?"

"Yes," I said pushing off the covers to show that I was serious. "Something light."

She nodded hesitantly before giving Miracle a set of instructions and leaving my room.

"Is there anything else you need Princess?" asked Miracle hopefully. I gained that she didn't like having nothing to do.

"Uhm, can I get something to drink as well?" How original. But it perked her up and with a bow she left the room.

David and I were alone at last. I couldn't stand looking this vulnerable with so many people about.

"Come closer," I said to him, gesturing to my side. He

looked uncertain and proceeded with caution.

"I won't bite," I joked but it seemed lost on him. He just plumped down on the seat by my bed and held his head in his hands, miserable.

"David?" I whispered worriedly. "David what's wrong?" His head jerked up suddenly.

"All of this," he sighed. "Increased protection; nonsense."

He laughed bitterly. I'd never seen him like this. Or was this part of the shock? "They breached the palace and were able to plant a bomb in one of the cars."

I blinked. It did seem kind of strange and then begged the question...

"David, how many attacks have there been on the palace in the past couple of months?" He raised an eyebrow.

"I don't know, quite a few; why"?

"Do they have anything in common?"

It felt stupid to ask, he was with me all the time I was in Sapele. If I didn't know something there was very little chance of him knowing it either. But it was safe to assume that he got reports or at least read a newspaper even though I wasn't allowed to.

He put his hand on his chin in thought while I stared at him.

"Well," he began eventually. "I used to get reports on attacks on the palace, but most of them seemed odd."

"Odd?" I said leaning forward.

"Most of them were definitely outside jobs but I think of others... like, this morning the sirens were on."

I scrunched my nose in confusion. "Why wouldn't they be?"

His eyes darkened suddenly, "The attack on the city last week where some rebels got into the palace; the siren was disabled."

My eyes widened. "But surely, the guards on duty would have seen them."

"Aria," David sighed his voice hoarse. "They were the guards on duty."

The world stopped for a minute.

"Somehow they had gotten hold of uniforms and had infiltrated the palace."

My mouth felt dry and wished that Miracle would come back with my water. If they were already in the palace who knows what kind of havoc they could create?

"They were found, mind you, before they could do any more damage."

He gulped nervously. I can't believe he had this weighing on his chest all week without mentioning it to me. Did he mention it to Ma Osa? She probably wouldn't have let me leave if she did. Only last week. And why hadn't we heard it on the news? Not that it would have mattered. There was only one family on our street with twenty-four hour electricity and it was not us.

"If you were here last week and they got a hold of you…," David muttered, his eyes not meeting mine. I placed my hand on his and he looked up.

"Hey, I'm still here you know, a little shaken but still here."

"Yes, today. But if…"

There was a knock at the door. David rose up and to my surprise it wasn't my maids. It was Alexander.

"I'd like to see my cousin," he stated firmly.

"I'm sorry, but the princess is not here."

I thought that was over until Alexander peeked past him and caught sight of me.

"Imotenya," he said, shoving past David and entering the room. Didn't he realise that this was the queen's bedroom? He stopped seeing that I was in bed wrapped in a blanket and tilted his head.

"Are you all right?" he asked although in the circumstances it should have been the other way round.

"I'm fine," I lied. "How's your father?" "Recovering," he replied, not inching a step closer.

"That's good." It was all I could come up with.

He just nodded and came to the side of my bed.

"Can I speak with you please, alone." He gestured to David who was watching him with narrowed eyes. I'd be a sorry excuse for a future queen if I couldn't even talk to my upset cousin without my guard present.

But if he's upset, then maybe it's a good idea that I'm not alone in his company.

"David, please," I said bravely. He tensed a little but then went into the sitting room and closed the door. I swear I could hear him breathing against the door.

Alexander took David's place beside my bed and looked around the room. It probably hadn't occurred to him that he was in the queen's chambers. I was wondering if he was even allowed in here, no matter his relationship to us.

"What is it that you wanted to talk to me about?" I said, trying not to sound frightened. Even though David was on the other side of the door, I felt on edge.

Apparently, I had no reason to be. Alexander just held his head, his hands, his shoulders trembling a little. I had never seen a man appear so weak.

He finally looked at me, his eyes like dark ice.

"Father was almost killed today in what looked like an attack on you, but thankfully he survived."

"Yes, he did," I said with a smile on my face but something was not right about this. Why wasn't he happy?

"Your mother doesn't trust my father." I looked at him.

"What?"

"You heard me," he replied bitterly. I'd never think him capable of such a look. He didn't give me a chance to reply before continuing.

"You think that the guys who attacked the palace did the bombing do you?"

I blinked. "Of course, maybe not the exact same people but... why wouldn't they be?"

A few seconds passed as he looked at the ceiling, then at the floor, then back at me with an aghast look before finally getting up.

"I should not have come. I'm sorry cousin, and I hope you feel better soon." He opened the door to the bedroom and didn't look back.

I heard the chamber door slam before I caught sight of the questioning faces of David, Hanna and Miracle. David was at my side in two strides.

"What did he want?" he asked. "Please, tell me."

I wanted to. I really did, but no words came out. How could you repeat something that wasn't said.

"He just wanted to check how I was doing," I said, forcing myself to smile even though my heart ached at leaving David in the dark about my cousin's suspicions which looking at them were ridiculous. Did he think that we were ones responsible for the bomb? My breath caught in my chest. Maybe he did?

My musings were interrupted as Miracle handed me a glass of water, Hanna placed a tray with fruit on my lap, while David went back to his place against the wall. Nothing out of the ordinary happened after that.

Chapter 13

I was restless later in the day even though I had stayed in bed for most of it. My mother managed to find time out of her hectic schedule to see me and then said that my aunties were very worried when they heard about the bombing and that they had spent most of the day hiding out in their rooms.

Somehow, I thought that they would rather be hiding out far, far away from the palace. I couldn't blame them for that however. If I had a choice or a life that was actually my own, I wouldn't stay here any second longer than I had to, not even for the food.

They expressed their thoughts when dinner came around, where my mother, uncle and cousin were not present.

"I am thinking of going back to Ibadan tomorrow," announced Auntie Osoye, breaking a piece of chicken leg. "Junmi, needs my help with her baby. Stupid girl, if she was going to have a child why did she decide to take on a fulltime job in the same year?"

"It's all these career girls, they don't have the intelligence to balance things properly," replied Auntie Ayela taking a sip of water.

They both stopped in the middle of their meal and looked at me. Was I supposed to say something?

Or was I as a female heir becoming my own brand of "career woman". I only realised then, that I didn't know that much of what my aunties thought of me ascending to the throne someday.

From what I saw at the table at least, they were of the generation that thought that a woman was supposed to stay at home and look pretty. And worse, they were from a rich enough background, that meant a woman wasn't supposed to do anything.

I was actually afraid to ask them what they thought.

"It would be best for us to leave anyway," said Auntie Ayela, looking a little more earnest this time. "Your mother is very busy."

I put down my spoon full of rice.

It didn't seem right. She was supposed to be mourning for her husband and yet she had to deal with attacks on her family and the complete upheaval our nation was in.

That will be you someday. I shook my head. I could not think of that now.

Both of my aunties left the table to go pack. They both gave me a hug and words of consolation. They were being as nice as they could be during the circumstances, at least, that was what I wanted to believe.

I sat there staring at the ceiling and its swirly bronze pattern. I wondered if it was an initial design. If the architect of this dining room had an idea of a complete product when he had and finished and ran with it. Or was it an experimentation process? The swirls on the left looked uneven: some were too wide while others took a different shape entirely. Or maybe that was the plan: to portray organized chaos. Much like what my life was turning out to be.

When I finally looked down, I had a crick in my neck and decided I should probably leave so that the maids could clean up. As I walked down to the hall to God knows where, I almost bumped into someone.

"I'm sorry Your Highness," they said with a bow. When they finally straightened up I recognised him immediately.

It was the boy from last night. The one I had knocked down.

"It's quite alright," I said, straightening my back. "Just don't make a habit of it while you're here." His eyes widened a little. I was surprised at myself in fact.

"Forgive me," he said now looking me in the eye. "But you're the one who bumped into me twice."

I was too exhausted and confused to be actually annoyed but still, I fixed him with a hard glare.

"Forgive me, but should you be... not in the way."

I could see from the mirth in his eyes that was present there yesterday that didn't border on insolence and yet was still respectful.

"I was going to the kitchen to get some tea for your uncle, Highness."

"Tea?" I was surprised, glad that my uncle was in a state to drink tea, but confused as to why he'd drink tea in this weather. Must be a Lagos thing.

"Yes," the servant replied. "It seems to calm him when he's anxious." I nodded solemnly. He must be more than anxious now.

"Well, if you'll excuse me, Your Highness, but I must get His Highness's tea."

"Oh, yes you must."

He moved to the side to get to the kitchens but I stopped him to ask, "Do you know where my cousin is?"

He thought about it for a minute then replied, "He took a tray in his room a few hours ago."

"Thank you…" I realised again that I hadn't caught his name.

"James, Your Highness."

James. An ordinary name for a servant and yet there was something about him. "Pleasure to meet you James," I said politely.

He just smiled and bowed before heading down to the kitchens. Now, I'd have to find my cousin and talk to him.

I went up the stairs to the guest rooms and hoped that he was in his room. There were guards at his door which after today made plenty of sense.

"I'd like to speak with my cousin please," I said. Before I had finished my sentence, the door opened to reveal a disheveled Alexander. He didn't look surprised to see me. In fact, I couldn't garner that much from his face.

"Oh," he said looking down at himself bashfully and ran a hand through his hair. "Come in." So, I did.

His room was a mess. Shirts and socks were hanging on the table and chair, sheets of crumpled papers littered the floor. His tray that had been brought up was left untouched on the floor and I caught sight of broken glass.

Something told me that James must not have been here at all today. He was too busy attending to my uncle. There was something about him that told me he wouldn't leave his master's room so unkempt.

"Sit down, sit down," he said, not looking at me. I wasn't sure where to sit so I settled at the edge of his bed and folded my hands in my lap.

He turned around slowly to face me.

"I'm sorry for the way I left earlier," he whispered looking like he was in a daze.

"It's fine," I replied. No one could fault him for that.

"I never got to finish what I said though," he continued as he began to pace back and forth slowly.

"How much do you really know about what's going on?"

"Excuse me?"

"I doubt that you were given anything to deal with besides books, I mean you're so young." What was he talking about?

He chuckled bitterly, putting a hand on his side before turning back to me. "And yet you're the cause of so much trouble."

My hands were shaking and regret coming here on my own. I should have at least come here with David.

"Things would be so much easier for you if my father was dead, both your parents knew that." I stopped squirming.

"That's not true," I said earnestly. It was true that my uncle was a key factor in my ascension, but that didn't mean that my parents wanted him… no they couldn't.

I tried to think of anything I had heard during the years. Anything at all, but it was useless. I was limited in what I could watch on TV, newspapers were hidden out of sight from me and hardly had that much contact with anyone outside my tutors and foster family.

"It would be easy though. They rebels are unsatisfied with the royal family in general so it wouldn't matter which member they killed. They could have hit Auntie O, for all they cared. They just want to make a statement."

He came and sat on the other side of the bed so that I couldn't see his face.

"But nobody would suspect anything if someone was killed after the palace was attacked."

"But nobody was killed," I implored, afraid of seeing his expression.

"But they could try again."

I snapped my head round and pulled his shoulders to face me.

"Look," I said desperately. "We all have been through a lot these past few days so just stop making these accusations okay? Just stop."

He pushed away my hands and said with his eyes as cold as black ice, "You're just like them." I was close to tears. And I didn't even know why.

I just got up, muttered an apology and a goodbye without reply, before I left my cousin's room, never looking back.

I didn't have any clue where I was going until I found myself in the medical wing. Face to face was my uncle laying in a bed, his head in a bandage and wrapped in a sterile white cloth, timidly sipping his tea with James and a doctor standing in the corner. Was it my fault he was like this? Not at death's door but almost?

I couldn't stand seeing him like this so I ran back the way I came. If there were servants present, they must have thought I had gone mad, running back and forth like this. I went up a flight of stairs and came to a long corridor not unlike any others I had seen in the palace after almost a day of lying down, I would have walked to Sokoto in order to clear my head. I pushed on the door to the right, it opened.

I'd expected it to be some guest room or maybe storage,

not what I saw in front of me.

It was an office, but as I looked around, I saw it wasn't just any office. It was the king's office.

Where Baba worked. Where I would work someday. It was mostly stripped down, to reflect the state of transition. I'd have to decide how to re-decorate it when the time came.

For now, I looked up at the static A.C, fingered through the filing cabinets and then sat at the chair by the desk. It was one of those ones that spun and made of thick expensive suede. It must have come from abroad. I tried to imagine Baba, sitting here. Maybe he spun around when he was alone and didn't want to deal with taxes or road complaints.

This chair to me seemed more important than the throne. The throne was just part of the ceremony. Like a wedding. The days spent sitting at this desk were the marriage.

I spun from side to side thinking of nothing at all until I saw a drawer in the desk. Inquisitively, I pulled at its handle. It wouldn't move. Strange. The cabinets were open. I looked again and noticed there was a lock on it. Not a regular lock though. It was straight.

I got up and searched for the key in every area in the room. I even stood on a chair to check the top cabinet and shelves. Note for when I'm queen: get shorter filing cabinets. I checked around the sides of the chairs and even in the mini-freezer which contained a six-set of Heineken.

Another note for when I'm queen: get better drink options.

In the end it was no use. I couldn't find my evasive key. Perhaps he took with him to his room. If it was important, he wouldn't have wanted just anyone having access to it. I huffed and fell back into the chair. So much for that.

I looked again at the desk and caught sight of what looked like a picture frame. I picked it up and stared while trying to hold back tears.

It was a picture of my father holding me in this very office. It seemed like he didn't carry me often because he was holding me awkwardly but I didn't seem to mind. He was laughing at my cheeky toothless smile. He was wearing a white shirt with a gold thread wrapper and I was wearing one of those pink onesies and missing one shoe. He didn't look like a king, a man in charge of many affairs and many people, he just looked like Daddy.

"Who's in here?"

I almost dropped the picture and scampered up but straightened up when I saw who it was. It was Mama who came into the office. Now I wished I hadn't intruded.

"I'm sorry, Mummy," I began in a hurry. "The door was open so I just…"

"It's all right." She put a hand to her head as if the very discussion was causing her pain. "

Are you fine? You weren't at dinner."

She just smiled fondly at me, directing me away from the desk.

"I am my dear, I just had some work to finish up on."

I just nodded but didn't fail to recognize how spaced out she seemed looking around Baba's room.

Even when we left and she shut the door behind her. She asked a guard to stand watch and when we went down the stairs, she never stopped looking back.

Chapter 14

I flipped through channels on the TV in Mama's room. Perhaps that's why one wasn't added to my room, so I wouldn't feel too bad about having to stay in my mother's bedroom at night. It would have worked if there was anything worthwhile on the television.

On trips to Mosalgar, where if you were lucky there was one television per neighbourhood, the moving pictures of superheroes running around were enough to astound anyone. Now, flipping through national and international channels, I just felt irritated — aghast; I just didn't care about what was on.

Mama's maid, Dessa, looked wary of my blank stare as she rearranged Mama's wardrobe. Even though no channel stayed on for longer than a second, she kept apologising when she had to pass by television to retrieve something from the other side of the room. I finally got up from my bed and looked through the stack of books that were on the nightstand. Two of them were folded at the top near the very start. I guess there wasn't much time for reading when you were queen which was a pity. The only way I was able to pass my tests was through my own reading. I could never concentrate when my tutors were around.

I pulled out an old hardback entitled, "Genealogy of Xavian Royalties, Volume 30". I skipped through the lengthy introduction and the ancestors who have long been pushing up the palm trees, and came to relatives I had actually heard of.

It turned out that my grandfather, King Jonathan, had two wives and fourteen concubines. My father was of course the eldest boy from the second wife, Queen Aresa. Uncle Lucky, was the second son. There were also other children from some concubines. I wondered what it would be like to be the son of some sort of male concubine. If there was a female harem, why not a male? I wonder if the lawmakers ever thought of that. Would that even bear worth thinking about? It seemed difficult to find one suitable man, not to talk of a few and that sort of thing just didn't interest me. Well, not including one man that I knew...

I shook my head and went back to looking through the book. I turned to Mama's family tree. She was the youngest of five children of her mother: two boys and three girls. Her father had six wives. She was the daughter of his second wife. Meaning Ma Osa's aunt was my mother's step-mother. It was funny how families go.

I looked further down and came a little closer to home. Prince Desmond married Beatrice Ikha and had two children. Me and my dead brother. I turned to Uncle Lucky's side and saw that he married a woman named Patience Oduwana, a chief's daughter and had Alexander and Patience.

I steadied my breath and looked around to see if I could find my cousin 'Best' but it was no use. I thought as much. That's why we used aliases. What wouldn't I give, to have my old pen-pal back.

That's when I realised. My letter to the girls. It was still on my table. With the bombing, I had forgotten to post the letter. I huffed, closed the book and went to my room. On the way, I ran into David who cursed himself for not being with me after dinner.

"I'm telling you we ate fast," I said. "And anyway, you don't have to be with me every second of the day."

"I sort of do, little dove," he replied sounding adamant. "Because..."

"I'm doing my bit for King and Country, young lady," I finished, drawing myself up to full height and mimicking his accent. It drew a shadow of a smile from David.

A shadow that retreated back from whence it came when we were at my room.

My beautiful room. It was trashed. The covers were torn open, clothes were splayed across the floor, the bookshelf was toppled and book pages were torn out. Behind me I heard David call out for some officers while I stood in the scene. I made my way to my desk where my tin of letters looked riffled through and crumpled and I saw that the letter I'd written was intact but there was a note left on the table, on brown paper that looked like if might have been used to wrap something beforehand, because there were splotches all over it.

It read: 'Be warned, we know your secret.' What secret?

I didn't realise that I wasn't alone until I was dragged out by Hanna and Miracle.

"Excuse me, Your Highness," said one of the guards whose name I didn't know or even care to figure out. "But we will need to question your maids."

I didn't answer. So David answered for me, by gently

pushing me away from my room leaving my maids with the guards. They must have taken my silence as a yes.

David kept his hands on my shoulders while he guided me back to Mama's room. I felt like I was going to be sick again. David sensed my distress and came in front of me. I didn't look up.

"Aria?" he whispered. I couldn't move. I didn't want to feel anything. So much had gone so wrong in so little time. What was the point of me coming back here? I just seemed to have made things worse for everyone involved.

"David," I murmured softly, starting to look up into his dark concerned eyes. He was the only thing in my whole life that I could count on. He was home. He was safe. "Can I have a hug?"

I felt so pathetic. My house was breached today, my uncle almost died, my father had died and here I was crying over a bedroom. I was a horrible human being.

David didn't say anything. He just pulled me towards him and wrapped his arms around me in a tender embrace. I buried my face into his guard's jacket and put my arms around his waist to steady myself. I didn't care that we were in the middle of the corridor, where anyone could see us, I didn't even consider anyone else. All I knew in that moment was the feel of David's breath against my neck and his hands running up and down my back. I didn't consider how this was for him. It might have been his job but it put him in harm's way as well and I couldn't lose him.

After a small eternity we parted.

"Better?" he asked, straightening his jacket with a soft smile.

I gave him an answer that would help us move on. "Yes, I am now."

He didn't seem to buy into it but he looked me in the eye with a determined gleam in his eyes. "We will find those responsible for this. All of it, I promise."

I let out a bitter chuckle. "Don't make promises you can't keep Officer."

He didn't say anything. He just bit his lip the way he did when he didn't have the words needed in any situation. His eyes were downcast and stormy. I hated seeing him like this.

"Hey," I said, taking his hand in mine. I noticed the calluses on his hands from his job on the farm. I took in his face, how it was so different from the boy I first met ten years ago, how I'd seen it smile, laugh, frown and everything else in between.

We shouldn't have stayed there. I'm sure he knew as well as I did that whoever did that to my room could still be about and that we needed to be on the move as soon as possible. But we still didn't move. Not until I stepped closer towards him. Without missing a beat, he wrapped an arm around my waist. Slowly, gently, he fingered my cheeks.

This was past breaking protocol. This was crossing an invisible line but somehow, we didn't care. My lips slowly parted as I pulled him as best as I could towards me. His thumb brushed against the corner of my lips with something I couldn't decipher in his eyes. It couldn't be longing could it? Before either of us could make another move, we heard footsteps coming towards us.

"Imotenya, where are you?"

It was Mama. We pulled apart clumsily as Mama came down the hall with Aisha trailing behind her. Her body might have been moving towards me, but her whole countenance was that of a dead woman. Did she really have to be here? She should be sitting down, quietly grieving for her husband not worrying about a threat against her child or her kingdom. And definitely not about the stupid accusations her nephew was making. But looking at it now, how stupid were those accusations? We still hadn't found out who was responsible for the bombing then. There was the destruction of my room. But why mine?

I'm sure there were other more valuable places in the palace to go to. And the note. It had to be an inside job. All of a sudden, my skin turned cold and not because of the A.C. A rebel had infiltrated the palace and they were out for blood.

I stepped into Mama's arms as we were guided back to the Queen's chamber where two more guards were patrolling. They seemed more tense and alert than ever. Did they believe as I did, that somehow someone had managed to sneak into the palace and in the worst case scenario, they were still here.

I suddenly remembered what David said about the rebels who had donned guard costumes in the past. At that, I invariably shook at the sight of the guards stationed at my mother's door. Had one of them been in my room and had left that note?

When we were in Mama's room, I went directly to my bed and took out the two pieces of paper I'd taken from my desk. I spread them both out in front of me as I sat cross-legged looking at them both in turn. Two very different specimens. One written out of love and the other...

I didn't know what it was written for. "Aria?"

I looked up from the letter and the note into the eyes of my guard who was standing in the doorway to the bedroom.

"I just wanted to check and make sure that you're alright."

I nodded slowly.

"I'm fine." Though I really wasn't. I had so many questions that needed answers and I wasn't sure who to ask to get the right answers. And for some pesky reason, I couldn't ask David because all that came up in my mind was that moment we shared in the corridor. Did he feel anything? Would he tell me if he did? Did I really want to know if he did? He just brought a hand to chin with a curt nod as he looked everywhere but my face.

"We don't believe you're in any real immediate danger but they're still looking out for well, anything."

I nodded again. It must be difficult to not know exactly what you're looking for.

Or exactly what you're feeling.

"They're going to talk to the guys in the cell, right?" I asked, it seemed like the most logical step forward.

"Yes," David replied now looking at me. "Again. I don't know, I just can't believe one group of people can be so desperate."

"You think it's someone else involved, don't you?"

He didn't say anything because we were interrupted by Mama's voice. "Officer, you may leave now if there isn't anything else."

We shook as if we were small children being reprimanded. David turned on his heel to leave.

"Wait," I said. He turned around expectantly while my hand hovered over the note to pick it up, but then I stopped suddenly. This was evidence wasn't it? I should be willingly handing it over to be able to catch whoever was responsible.

But I just couldn't.

"What is it?" David asked, not looking that anxious about overstaying his welcome. I gulped. Then took a breath. Then smiled.

"Thank you for everything."

He looked down bashfully as if not used to receiving such thanks then he straightened, looking more like the honourable guard that he was.

"Just doing my job, Aria."

"Well, for the parts that are not your job."

It was my turn to feel abashed. He just smiled in a way that didn't help my raging thoughts and made all my senses come alive with a vivacity that they hadn't known before.

He bowed and left the queen's bedroom.

Later when I'd go to sleep, I'd think of the way he held me, making me forget that I was in a place where everything was not as it seemed.

Chapter 15

Seeing my aunties leave produced a mixture of emotions. On one hand, I was glad to see the eccentric women leave and be out of harm's way; on the other hand, that left me the company of a grieving mother, an incapacitated uncle and a hateful cousin.

"Madams!" Aisha was running at full speed, waving plane tickets in her hand. I shouldn't forget the ditzy secretary.

Auntie Osoye and Auntie Ayela were standing in front of one of the cars to take them to the airport. I always found it odd that it was only for domestic flights, the nation's international airport was in the south-west. Maybe, it was some sort of security measure.

Auntie Ayela hugged me and my cousin at least twice while Auntie Osoye was in a deep conversation with Mama. I couldn't make out what she was saying, as I was once again pressed into the chest of Auntie Ayela.

"My girl," she said. "I hope we'll meet again. Now you take care of your mother, okay?"

I couldn't answer properly, I was fully pressed against her impressive bosom. Did constant drinking provide supernatural strength? Out of the corner of my eye, I saw Alexander staring at me with an armor-piercing expression. What was he trying to do?

Auntie Ayela let me go eventually and transferred her onslaught onto Alexander. Auntie Osoye called me over to give her a hug which was much shorter than those of Auntie Ayela's.

"Don't cause your mother any trouble, you hear. She's got a lot on her plate." I wanted to roll my eyes but that would be seen as disrespectful, but then she whispered. "Take care of yourself, so far I can see that you've been doing well enough already." Although I knew that a great many people had been involved in how far I had gotten, I couldn't help but feel a little touch of pride, especially coming from someone like Auntie Osoye.

"Thank you, Auntie," I said as we pulled back. Maybe I had misjudged her.

She smiled then went and then complained of how Auntie Ayela was in the front seat and nobody respected their elders these days, but eventually was seated in the back.

We waved goodbye until they were through the palace gates, Mama waving a little while after that. I made my way back into the palace but, unfortunately, Alexander had the same idea.

"After you," I said, trying to sound cordial. He just shrugged and entered making a beeline to the medical wing. I just sighed and went up the stairs to Mama's room. My room had been cleared out early that morning, but I was in no rush to go back there and I was even in less of a rush to see who was coming in front of me. My uncle's servant James. He was carrying a basket of clothes from my cousin's room and almost didn't see me.

I didn't see anywhere I could duck, so I kept on walking. Unfortunately, he saw me and tried to bow but failed and ended up spilling all his master's clothes on the floor, blocking my path.

"I'm so sorry, Your Highness," he stuttered immediately getting on his hands and knees to pick up the clothes.

I instinctively got down with him and put some of the clothes back in the basket. "You don't have to do this," he said so unlike the cheerful boy I had met the last two times. "Please, don't tell me what I don't have to do," I replied, pulling a handkerchief from under my knee. "I get enough of that already."

He looked casually at a spot on the floor. "I'm sorry, highness."

I chewed on my bottom lip and was lost in thought. James was close enough to my cousin that he sorted out his clothes. That didn't mean Alexander talked to James over beers but it did mean that James might have been privy to a sudden outburst, an implicit remark, a cryptic conversation, anything I could find out about Alexander.

We got up slowly and I decided to take the plunge.

"James..." That's when I realised I didn't know exactly what to say. I couldn't just ask him "Why does your master's son believe my mother wanted to kill his father? If anything, they should be trying to kill me, which they probably are." No, I needed to be more tactful.

"How is Alexander keeping, with his father, I mean?"

James hefted the basket to a more comfortable position and seemed to ponder my question. "He is very upset," he began. "But I'm sure with His Highness's improvement, he will feel much better."

Not the answer I was exactly looking for, so I'd have to dig deeper.

"Horrible thing to have happened here isn't it," I said gauging his reaction. "And to think it could have been any of us."

"'Us' meaning the royal family?"

I stopped. When he put it like that, I realised that I didn't know that much else about the bombing. I had been assuming that my uncle was the only victim of the bombing when there must have been others in the compound. Innocents. I couldn't stomach the thought, but somehow, I continued.

"It was quite a shock, especially after the rebels had been caught earlier coming into the palace."

"I suppose so."

This was much more difficult than I had anticipated. It was going to take much more than a brief conversation in the corridor to get this across and I could see that James looked a bit uncomfortable still carrying the basket.

"James, do you happen to have an hour off, say at two?"

He looked a little startled but replied, "It depends on how much I can get done before then, and if His Highness needs me."

I nodded. Of course, which meant I needed to let him go right away.

"Well, if you can meet in…" I paused. Where could we meet that didn't look suspicious. I didn't know anywhere.

"Might I suggest the library," said James.

"Yes, the library," I said as if I knew that was the obvious answer. I never knew we had a library not to talk of where it was.

"So at the library at two, Your Highness?"

"See you there then."

None the wiser, he forfeited the bow and just lowered his

head until I had walked past feeling a little hopeful. Maybe later I'd get some answers, but for now I'd ...

I stopped. I didn't know what I was going to do until then. The day before yesterday was my arrival, and yesterday I had a near brush with death and this morning my aunties had left the palace. I had yet to get accustomed to normal life. So I just went back to doing what I did in Sapele. Studying.

When I got back to my room, I saw none other than Petal rearranging my bed.

"Petal!" I ran to her, almost startling the poor thing and pulled her into an embrace. I know I had only known her for less than two days, but that didn't mean I didn't miss her quiet presence and the diligent way she worked. With Hanna's matron-manner and Miracle an overeager puppy attitude, Petal was a calm wave in between.

I finally let go and smiled at her. She looked surprised and then smiled straightening my dress in case it had been crumpled.

"Good Morning Your Highness," she said. I hadn't realised but she didn't do a lot of greetings. That was mostly Hanna or sometimes Miracle. Perhaps being on her own gave her a certain surety, that she wouldn't be compared to her colleagues.

"How are you feeling?" I quickly asked. Was she in any condition to be working?

"Much better Princess," she replied then looked down as if suddenly aware of something wrong. "I'm sorry about my absence and thank you for letting me keep my job."

"That's ridiculous," I scoffed, taking her hands. "You weren't fit to work and needed a break, that's all." I knew it

114

was much more than that, but there was no use dwelling on the past.

"And besides, with everything going on, we don't have the time to look for another maid, right?" I hoped she would see reason. And she did. Well, she appeared to. I went to my desk and took out my notepad as well as undamaged book on military warfare, sat down but before I could get into things I had to ask;

"Petal, do you know where the library is?"

Sure enough, she did. It wasn't complicated at all. Turns out it was on the bottom floor at the very back of the palace. When I saw it, I couldn't understand why. There were chaises with silver legs, the high shelves were lined with gold and there was a huge window that gave a full view of the gardens. The walls were lined with bronze horns and lamps, while each of the mahogany tables had ivory runners down the middle. The ruby red thick curtains were pulled back by gold chords, which if needed, afforded much privacy.

I fell back into a recliner and closed my eyes. Why hadn't I found out about this place earlier? I could have saved myself a great deal of headaches by having somewhere peaceful where I could relax.

"Your Highness?"

My eyes snapped open at the familiar voice. James was coming carrying a handful of books. I rose up to help him. He thanked me as we set them down on a table in the corner of the library. "It was a good excuse to come here," he said, his usual mirth returning. "To return these and make sure I hadn't mixed them up with Master Alexander's personal ones."

I admired his shrewdness, but still regretted that he had to be dishonest with his boss. I looked at the covers of the books and saw that they were very varied. One was a copy of 'Great Expectations' another was one on astronomy while a huge hardback was 'A Great Awakening: A study in the Mind.' Alexander was not a man of limited interests.

James and I sat opposite each other, careful not to be soaked into the cushy chairs. I took a deep breath and tried to form a coherent sentence in my mind.

"There's no rush, Your Highness," James said looking a little tense all of a sudden. I hoped it wasn't because of me and almost felt guilty because of his concern.

"Well I don't know where to begin," I admitted wringing my hands and trying my best to fight the urge to just walk out.

"I believe it had something to do with the bombing Princess," James said politely.

"Aria," I blurted out suddenly. "Call me Aria." It wasn't my given name, like 'Imotenya' but it was the name I responded to the most. What actually felt like me. It felt weird to be sharing it with him.

He just blinked then quickly resumed his nonchalant posture.

I decided to go on. "Yesterday, Alexander remarked that he didn't believe that the bombing was caused by outsiders but was arranged by the queen."

James's shoulders visibly slumped and a worried expression took hold of his face. I didn't know whether I should be glad or disappointed at that look.

"He was very upset at what happened to his father. He may not have meant it."

I had thought of that especially looking at the entire

situation we were in, but something told me that there was more to it.

"He hasn't expressed anything, anything at all, that show he thinks this." James paused and thought carefully. I don't know what I was hoping he would say. "Nothing I can think of."

I chewed the insides of my mouth in frustration. I really thought I was onto something here.

"Master Alexander has always seemed to love his aunt as well as his uncle," James said. "When we heard the news on the way here, he was devastated. They must have been close." Something in my stomach churned hearing that. First Alexander and now his servant, boasting about how close Alexander was to the king. It was sickening. I had always thought that they would keep Uncle Lucky's family at double arm's length. But here they were with their close relationship. While they sent their own child away. Why be afraid of the enemy if you're going to end up fraternizing with them anyway?

"Aria, are you all right?" I looked at my hands and noticed that I was gripping on the chair handle. I felt the leather fibers seep into my fingernails. I let go immediately.

"Sorry, I was distracted," I mumbled looking at my nails.

"It's fine," said James. "If it's all right, I think Master Alexander will be wondering where I am."

I looked at the time. We hadn't been here that long but technically he was supposed to be working. And I had wasted enough of his time already.

"Of course," I said, getting up and dusting off my dress. It had become a bad habit lately.

"I'm sorry I couldn't be that much help," James said rising

to his feet and placing his hands in his pockets. "But, if you ever need to talk, I'm here."

I stood surprised. I wasn't expecting him to be so receptive. I was basically trying to dig up dirt on his boss. The lack of answers could have been from sheer loyalty but somehow, I didn't think so. His loyalty couldn't go as far as treason could it?

"Thank you, James," I said. I'm sure he wouldn't. I left him to his work and left the library, feeling I had just taken two steps back.

Chapter 16

Uncle Lucky was making a steady recovery. He was back to his characteristic charismatic self. Alexander was with him all afternoon. Maybe now he'd be less sour. But Mama would be tenser. I wanted to believe all would be well but I couldn't stop thinking of how Alexander might have been right: that, somehow, mother was responsible for the bombing. But if she wanted Uncle Lucky dead, surely, she could have found an easier way to do it instead of endangering the lives of innocents… I had to stop thinking about that. There were more important things in front of me than court intrigue. There was my whole future to consider.

Now that Baba was gone, Mama reigned in his stead and would do so until her death or until I was deemed fit to rule which I hoped was in the distant future.

But preparation started today. My tutoring sessions were cut down to fewer hours so I could spend more time at Mama's side learning. It was nice that she did most of her work in her room, so I didn't need to move around so much. And at worse, run into Alexander who had still managed to avoid me.

"Imotenya, are you done with that paper yet?" asked Mama holding her hand out expectantly.

"Uhm, almost," I stuttered, clumsily handing back to her.

119

Today, Mama was going through more papers, while I blotted the ones that needed stamps. A very unstimulating job but actually it got me to see what the kingdom was actually dealing with: increased taxes, proposed roadworks, border disputes and so on and so forth. Personally, the roadworks should have taken full priority. Lagos road had been a myriad of potholes and deaths since before I was born. If five times the paperwork had not been on rebel activity, that situation would warrant immediate consideration.

As I stamped the royal seal on page after page, I caught sight of one that drew my attention. Words such as 'libel', 'defamatory' and 'treason' were used. I sought to look closer but a letter asking for an audience with the queen was quickly placed on top of it. All I could think about were the ominous words. Treason. It was a capital offence, but you wouldn't know it from the way Mama barely looked at it.

An hour passed as we went through today's file. Before Mama got up and said that we were done for now. My tutor wouldn't be here for another hour so I had some time for myself, but still, I couldn't stop thinking about that paper on treason. So I asked Mama about it.

"Oh, it's nothing," she said dismissively arranging her desk.

"If it's nothing, why's it on the queen's desk," I replied, moving to face her.

"I don't just get official letters Imotenya, some of them are personal and sometimes personal can be just that: personal." She slammed a book down on the table and I jumped. What had I done wrong?

She didn't say anything after that, but just kept packing up her filing box. I bowed and left the room to avoid another confrontation, but just as I moved to leave, I saw her riffle through the sheets I had stamped and pulled out the offending letter. Without flinching, she tore it into pieces

I sat on the terrace drinking lime-water, looking beyond the palace wall. Even though the palace was in the heart of the city surrounded by markets and packed streets, being here felt like a tranquil island. At least from the outside that's what it seemed. With suspicions and conspiracy theories and attacks floating around, I could have been on a never-ending motorbike ride. That's why I was sitting with legs outstretched watching David and some recruits, train down below. It was his day off and Officer Avril was taking his place by the terrace doors but as much as I more than abided him I couldn't help but watch my guard running in the midday sun. The palace must have had a gym but who would want to be inside on a day like today. And besides, it gave me the guilty pleasure of seeing my guard in a new light.

Believe me, I tried to concentrate on the vines growing along the walls, or the guavas in the trees that seemed ripe and ready to eat but try as I might, my gaze always reverted to focused eyes, tenses muscles and the perfect edges of his body. He had since removed his shirt; something I didn't remember him doing often. It wasn't uncommon for men to go around the house or even outside shirtless, but David was exceptionally modest. It was probably for a good reason though. I used to tease him mercilessly along with the other guards that came saying that he looked like a stick. But now he didn't. He looked beautiful. An ethereal blend of grace and power and...

I downed my glass of lime water to stop my overheating

body. I needed to stop thinking of him like that. He was old enough to be my uncle. It wouldn't end well for either of us.

"Princess?" Avery's voice said from inside.

I sat up and saw that Aisha was there standing beside him. She had on another pair of improbable heels which was rolled back and forth on.

"Good afternoon," I greeted getting up. From my lounge chair. Mainly so I wouldn't have the distraction down below distracting me.

"Good afternoon, Imotenya," she replied looking at some sort of checklist. "Don't forget your tutor will be here soon, so you don't miss that. All right honey?"

"Of course." Was she becoming my alarm clock now, as well as Mama's? She had a hand in most of what Mama did. Even her papers...

"Auntie Aisha," I said before she could turn away. I smiled brightly and took her hands shaking. "Thanks for coming to remind me of my lesson," I said, my voice soft as butter. She looked still shocked at this new sweetness but quickly brushed it aside and regained her chipper demeanor. As I hoped she would.

"I just wanted to ask if you look through the files that Mama's that gets in the morning?"

"Me?"

I almost thought I hit a nerve so I backed up a little. "Oh of course not..."

"I assure you Princess," she said a little too defensively as she flipped through her file. "Anything that arrives for the queen is for the queen's eyes only."

She said that as if reminding herself, but I couldn't stop

there. "Auntie Aisha, are there copies of the papers the queen receives?"

"Not to my knowledge. Unless the queen herself requested it." And in that case, I would have no business seeing them.

"Oh, that's all right," I said trying to hide my disappointment. How was I going to find out what that letter was about? It was torn to pieces.

But not thrown away. I didn't have a watch, but I knew I had some time left before my tutor got here. I had to see if they were still there. Without a word to Aisha or Avery, I dashed back inside and ran to the Queen's suite.

Once there I saw that it was empty. I checked inside the bedroom. No one was there, not even a maid on duty. I made a beeline towards the silver-plated desk and saw that the file was still there. She couldn't have put the pieces back into the file, could she? Nevertheless, I checked and sure enough they weren't there. I checked the drawers which thankfully were unlocked: no sign at all I looked around the desk. Nothing. I leaned back against the desk until I caught sight of the wastebasket in the corner. I went over to it. It hadn't been emptied yet.

Without a second thought, I dumped the contents onto the floor. I rummaged through seeing if I could find any piece of the latter. I found two, eventually, and scampered from the third piece until I heard the door. I paused then snapped back up as Mama's maid Dessa came into the bedroom holding a broom. I gripped the pieces of the letter in my hand. I did not want to know how I looked like standing with my hands guiltily behind my back and in front of an overturned bin. I felt at least two years old.

I didn't wait for a greeting or an explanation, I dashed out of the room leaving behind a very confused and work-weary Dessa.

"Princess, there is only one answer to number seven pay attention," sighed Mr. Zach, circling said question and handing it back to me before he went back to his own seat. I bit the top of my biro and scratched my leg looking at the question again, but I couldn't concentrate. Sure, I had gotten two pieces of the letter but the third was still back there. Actually, it wouldn't be there if Dessa had anything to do with it. I felt the other two pieces in the bottom of my shoes scuff my toes. I was itching to get out of this maths lecture and read those pieces. Honestly what was the point of this? It wasn't like I was going to use sine, cos or tan to tell me how hot I am! Or what direction the rebels were coming from. I crossed out my former answer and put down some random numbers before handing it back up. He barely glanced at it before giving me an incredulous look. I shrugged sheepishly. It was a miracle he had gotten through five years of being my maths tutor without strangling me out of annoyance. He couldn't really do that because I was royalty, but that didn't mean condescending retorts and looks were off limits though. I pitied any normal child who had him as a teacher. He looked like somebody who beats. Hard.

He just shook his head and wrote out the solution. He gave it to me with a mumbled "I'll see you next tomorrow." I nodded then left with Avery following behind.

The thing with Avery was that I could almost forget that he was in the room, even though among the guards I knew, he was the most jovial and talkative, I always seemed to be less aware of him than I was of David. The thought of him sent my skin prickling. Couldn't think of that now, had to get somewhere where I could read that letter. I remembered the library just down the hall.

"Thank you, Avery," I said. "I can carry on from here now."

His brows furrowed in uncertainty. "Are you sure, Highness?" he said, coming closer. "Someone is supposed to keep an eye on you at all times."

I wanted to roll my eyes. As if I didn't know that already. "I'll just be in the library going over my lessons."

He thought about it for a minute. "All right," he replied resignedly.

"Besides," I said. "There are guards stationed nearby."

He nodded, but he didn't turn around until I had gone into the library. I went back to the library and found a cushioned bench. I sat down drawing my knees up to my chest. I removed my shoe and unfolded the pieces of the letter. I arranged them in front of me like some obscure puzzle. I began to read...

To Her Majesty Beartrice Ighohemena Ikha Accra,

Regarding the matter you have asked of me in the past, I regret to inform you that there is no other answer to the question you once posed. It's a law that is as ancient as the first-born male...

The sentence was cut off.

Such an action, if it were to be revealed, would be considered treason and be defamatory to the entire royal family.

I stopped. If Mama didn't allow me to see this for fear that I would be frightened, she was completely right. I was frightened. I looked at the date on the letter. Written the day I had arrived. The day of the King's death. So Mama would have asked whoever had sent this a letter before that. But why? What did Mama need to know so badly, and why did she not want me to see it…

"Good Afternoon, Aria."

I jumped up letting the pieces fall to the ground. I rushed to pick them up but the intruder had the same idea. I looked up and saw that it was James.

"Sorry for scaring you," he said, taking hold of a piece of the letter. I moved to stop him touching his wrist.

"It's all right," I replied. He just nodded and looked down bashfully. I saw that my hand was still on his wrist quickly removing it before picking up the pieces of the letter and scrunching them in my hand.

"I just wasn't expecting anyone," I said trying to monitor my heart rate.

"I understand," said James. "I can leave."

He turned to leave, but I held him back.

"No, it's fine, it's just…" I stopped, when I realised I was taking his hand again. I let go then fell back on the bench and drew an arm across myself.

"Sometimes, I wish things were different. That I hadn't had my life planned for me and that I wasn't some puppet on a string. I wish things didn't have to change."

I felt pathetic. First, I burst into tears in front of this boy, then I asked him stupid questions and now I'm laying myself bare in front of him. And the worst part of it was, it was just so easy. Think of the irony. A servant of my enemy.

I looked down at my hands when I heard James' footsteps come closer then stop.

"I know what you mean," he said. "It was strange leaving home and working for the Prince and even stranger coming here. Change can be scary."

I looked up at him standing there with a wistful gaze in his eyes. I didn't know anything about him and yet he had seen me at my most vulnerable points.

"Why did you become the prince's servant?" I asked, gesturing to the space beside me. He cautiously moved over and sat in a way that there was a generous amount of space between us. "I kind of need the money," he began, "I applied for a position in the household, kitchen boy, gardener something like that but then I got to be Alexander's valet."

"That meant that I had to travel with him. I didn't even know we were going to the palace."

I nodded. I remembered Uncle saying something about being on his way to Beni before he even heard the news. I can definitely understand how James felt, moving from one uncertain position to another.

"But after some time, the changes don't seem so bad." Then he looked at me and almost winced. "But it doesn't compare to anything you must be going through."

I swallowed. "It kind of does. I was sent away from here when I was little and then I had to come at the worst possible time and now I don't know what happens next."

He nodded and slightly reached out his hand and drew it back. This was so hard. I was a princess which meant we couldn't be friends but if we were, well, I believed we'd get on.

"I think it's better that we don't. If we saw too far down

the line, we'd drive ourselves crazy. You can only deal with what's in front of you at any given time."

I chuckled bitterly. "What if so much is in front of you?"

I liked that he didn't rush to give me an answer. He placed an elbow on his knee and touched his chin before saying, "I'm sure you'll find a way. You were born for this."

I smiled. A real one this time. It was flattering to know somebody actually believed in me.

Before I could thank him the doors to the library swung open. We both got up and saw David coming through the door.

"Aria," he said. "Your mother's looking for you." He stopped and looked at James who started to seem a bit out of place here.

"I have some books to get for Alexander," he said, already backing away to the other side of the library, but not without a bow.

"Good day, Your Highness." I was disappointed that he was so formal all of sudden, as if the past few minutes didn't even exist.

"Aria?" David said breaking me out of my thoughts. I didn't say anything and just left the library with David following close behind.

After a few miniscule seconds, David asked, "Was that Alexander's servant?"

"Yes," I replied, straightening my dress since I was going to see the queen.

"That's interesting," my guard muttered. I quickly turned to him.

"What was?"

"Nothing really, I just saw the way he looked at you that's all." I blinked.

"What way."

David sighed as if the answer was clear as the nose on my face. "He seems to like you that's all."

I wrinkled my nose. "Who? James?"

"Ah, so that's what his name is."

I folded my arms across my chest. What was he getting at? "I have no idea what you're talking about."

He slowed his strides to come in step with me and smirked.

"Aria, I was that age once, I know what a guy looks like when he likes a girl."

I looked down at my feet all of a sudden and wondered if David would have liked me if he was my age? I liked to believe the answer was yes.

"I don't think so," I said dismissively. "Besides, he's not my type."

"Oh, aren't you a little too young to have a type?"

He said this was a joke, but I sensed a hint of disapproval.

"Well, I can't say exactly, I don't know him that well of course."

He nodded and for a minute I thought he was going to ask when was the first time I had spoken to him, until we got to our destination. The dining room. That was odd. The routine was mainly breakfast and dinner with the family and if we wanted anything for lunch, we'd ask the kitchens. Then it struck me. Maybe Dessa had told her about the bin and she got suspicious. I panicked. What would she say? What would I say? That I knocked over the bin?

I just opened the door and saw Mama sitting at the end of the table looking at more papers.

"Imotenya?" she said not looking at me. "Have you eaten yet?"

"No Ma," I replied. "Not yet."

She looked up and gestured to a maid in the corner who quickly bowed and went on her way to the kitchens.

I walked to Mama's side and sat next to her. Neither of us said anything. The incriminating letter pieces burned my feet as I looked at her from the corner of my eye. She had on her reading glasses and looked highly concentrated on whatever she was reading. I wondered if it was another letter from whoever sent the last one...

"Imotenya, tomorrow, there will be a parade." My head jerked up.

"A parade Ma? What for?"

She removed her glasses to look at me properly.

"To celebrate your return." She said that as if she was celebrating a dead rat's birthday. I clasped my hands. "Thank you, Mama."

"It's all been arranged," she went on. "A car will take us at ten tomorrow and we will go around the city."

Now I was a little more excited at the prospect. It had been years since I had been around the city. Sure, it would be in the back of a heavily guarded, heavily armoured car but it was better than nothing.

If only that letter was in the bottom of my shoe, this moment wouldn't feel so heavy. "And another thing. I think it is high time we went to see your uncle."

"Which uncle?"

"His Highness," Mama replied impatiently slamming down her pen. "Later in the day." Then she turned to David.

"Officer Soro, you will accompany us to the prince's quarters."

"Yes, Your Majesty," he replied compliantly.

The heaviness came back in full measure.

Chapter 17

Uncle Lucky had been moved back to his chambers so that's where we were going. I went to my room beforehand with the excuse to change and I put the letter pieces in my biscuit tin.

Hopefully my room wouldn't get raided again before I came back.

Uncle's room was on the second floor that was reserved for guests or extended family members. His room was in the centre of the hall which was carpeted in a lighter shade of red. I didn't know what to expect. I hoped against hope that Alexander wasn't present.

David pressed my shoulder gently. It would have been more comforting if I was actually sure what I was worried about.

There were guards stationed outside my uncle's room as well. The guards knocked and James answered. He bowed at the sight of the princess and the queen then stepped aside to let us in. When I looked around, the room looked so bare. There were the essentials, nothing more. No homely trinkets. If my uncle had any desire for the throne, wouldn't he have made his room in the palace seem more like home?

When I saw him, he was sitting directly under the A.C staring out the window with a glass in his hand with his head still bandaged.

"Dear sister," he said cheerfully raising his glass. One wouldn't know he had been injured in a bombing accident.

"Lucky," said Mama moving towards him sitting down on a chair James pulled out, "How are you feeling?"

This question, though well-intentioned, held an ominous air especially if Alexander was right.

"Ah," sighed Uncle leaning back in his chair, "So, so."

He pointed to the whirring A.C above. "This is a help. You know half the people only go to church because of one of these."

I snuffed a laugh. That was true. You always saw some straggler who fell asleep during the service, right under the A.C.

Mama chuckled a little and gestured for me to sit down at her feet. Apparently, I didn't need a chair. I was still only a child.

Uncle turned to me and grinned. "So how have you been my dear?" he said leaning forward to get a better look at me.

"I've been well," I said leaning back, trying to make myself comfortable on the floor. You would think sitting on the floor would be nice if it was in the palace.

"I hope Alexander has been nice to you," he said that nonchalantly as if he had no idea about his son's insinuations about my family. I scolded myself. Of course he didn't know. Otherwise, he would have been on the next plane out of here. Or maybe he was afraid his plane would be hijacked. That was a very real fear. I mentally slapped myself. If and only if those accusations were true.

So I said through gritted teeth, "Yes, he has."

He nodded. "That's good. Maybe you'll meet Patience at the burial huh,"

I wrinkled my nose. Who was Patience? Another cousin. Nobody ever knows how many cousins one has. You just run into new ones at every family event and even then, you couldn't be expected to remember their names. So why did the name Patience ring a bell?

"We have decided to have a parade tomorrow," Mama said. "To celebrate Imotenya's return."

"Oh, that's a very good move: to show the people that the princess is safe."

I noticed the way he used princess instead of heir. As if that was all he could ever see me as. Mama must have picked up on this as well because she said, resolutely "The people should be ready to meet their future queen."

Uncle grimaced but when I looked closely it seemed like it was from the pain. So James came over with a cushion and propped up my uncle's back and then gave him a glass of what appeared to be whisky. Uncle took it and downed it in one gulp. James went back to his corner of the suite. It was amazing to see that he knew what my uncle needed without him saying a word. And he'd only been working for him for what, a couple of weeks? He was very astute and I was a little disappointed to see him go. "Sorry, Sister," said Uncle, "But you know what they say, little something for the stomach."

Mama nodded obviously not getting his humour.

"Are you well enough to come to the parade?" I asked, trying to steer the conversation but after feeling a knee in my back, I had come to regret that decision.

"Ah," he said scratching his beard, "I'm not so sure I'm up for all the festivities just yet, but maybe Alexander would take part and ride in the back."

I nodded, hoping that we wouldn't have to sit too close to each other. "Besides as soon as I get better, I have to see Mariad Okode."

"The Royal record keeper?" Mama asked, raising an eyebrow. "Why would you need to see him?"

My interest was piqued. So that was who Uncle needed to see when he heard about Baba's death.

Uncle scratched his beard again before replying, "He has some old papers for me, nothing important, but I wanted to see them for myself."

She nodded but didn't seem so sure that was all. I didn't know what to think? For some reason I believed him. He was still a prince. He could travel anywhere he liked in the country.

After a few lighter topics and a bit of reminiscing of baba, Mama announced that we were leaving. I was glad to move my body to a more natural position.

We said our goodbyes before James opened the door to let us leave. Our eyes met for a moment but it was broken almost as quickly as I started. I turned and saw that David had been looking at James with a hard look. I brushed the side of his hand to tell him to stand down. He wasn't a threat.

Mama was going back to her to work and I was to accompany her. A ruler's job is never done so it seemed. When we were back at her desk, I saw that she didn't even look at the majority of the papers.

"Mama, what are those?" I asked stamping a letter to a florist.

She looked at the letters in question and just pushed them back into an envelope. "They are documents on the issues of state," she said plainly looking at another letter. "So why aren't you looking at them?" I asked, still keeping the stamp in the ink.

"The issues there will be discussed at the meeting with the chiefs," she replied plainly. She pulled at a silver chain around her neck.

"Don't you want to look at them before the meeting?"

"I already have." Her eyes snapped up to meet mine and I knew that I was to stop asking questions. I stamped the letter as she sighed and took my hand in hers. I saw the grief and fatigue and stress in her eyes that couldn't help but say, "I'm sorry."

I just smiled at her.

When I went to my room at the end of the day, I took off my shoes as I flopped onto the new bed that was put in my room. In a perfect world, I'd stay there until I fell asleep. But it wasn't and I was just there to pick up my sleeping clothes before going back to the queen's bedroom. Even after everything that had happened in the past few days, I wanted nothing more than to sleep in my own room. Perhaps I would when Uncle was well enough to leave. I grimaced. But it was not just him that we worried about, not anymore.

I stretched like the cat that used to come through the kitchen window in Sapele. Once Winter brought it into the house and managed to hide it under our bed, feeding it with biscuits and milk. After a couple of days, Ma Osa found it and threw it out of the house. Winter was devastated. I smiled bitterly. Maybe I could write her a letter asking her to try and hide me under the bed for the next couple of years.

I began to turn the letter pieces in my hand as I stared at

the ceiling. Why did Mama not want anything to do with this letter? I turned it around and noticed there was some small print. I looked closer and read the words 'Mariad Okode Royal Record Keeping office'. I had heard Uncle Lucky mentioning something about that earlier. That was where he was going when he came to Beni. To see some old papers. They couldn't have anything to do with whatever Mama had asked of the record keeper. Something that had to do with treason. I shivered as if it was harmattan in Jos. I shook my head, if it was important, I'm sure I would have been told.

That's what I kept telling myself, to force any hope of believing it to be true. I got off my bed and opened my biscuit tin, placing the letter pieces at the bottom. I was taking it with me tonight. I couldn't stand the thought of it being here anymore. I glanced at the letter on the top and something caught my eye.

I took it out. It was the first letter Best sent to me. I skimmed through it again as if it was the only thing that made sense in this crazy time. One line stood out. 'Patience is crying because I won't let her write in my letter.' Patience. Patience.

Uncle Lucky had children called Alexander and Patience. I was stunned when I understood. Out of all the cousins that I had, Best had to be Alexander. I slumped against the foot of the bed at that. The son of the man I had been sent away to protect, had been sending me letters this entire time. Did his father know? How did he find out the address? I bent over trying to get my breathing back to a normal pace.

Best was Alexander? Alexander was Best?

It was hard to believe. Why on earth didn't he say anything?

My head was tucked into my chest so deep that I was

worried it would leave a dent in my chest. I didn't hear the door opening. I didn't hear Petal come in. I didn't hear what she said to me. I just saw Ma Osa's scarf in her hands. She handed it to me and buried my face in it as if it was a life line, as she led me to the queen's room.

Chapter 18

We were at the bottom of the corridor waiting for Mama to arrive. We being Aisha, Alexander, Best whoever he was, and myself with a plethora of guards including David.

I didn't get a chance to talk to Alexander. He took his breakfast in his room again. Injured father or not, he was being a terrible house guest. He goes about raising suspicions about my family then sulking about. What was the point of him still being here anyway? What happened to the boy who used to write about how he really wanted to meet me and never spared any details on his life? He must have disappeared when he decided not to reply to my last letter.

I leaned back against the wall earning a disapproving glance from Aisha.

"Stand up straight, Your Highness," she said, coming over to adjust me. "You'll ruin the look of the dress."

I bit the inside of my cheeks to stop myself from saying anything I might regret. I trusted her to think more about the dress than me. It was a lovely dress to be honest. A deep maroon with stripes and a dark ruffle at the waist. I was wearing a gold bead crown. What would have made this outfit even better would have been a smile on my face. One that didn't even come on when Mama came down the stairs in a dress that matched mine. She said a few words to Aisha as the doors were opened and we were led to the car. It was similar to the one I came in but the top was off. Bold move.

Mama got in first then I slid in next to her. Aisha came in to sit in front of her, flipping vicariously through her notepad. Alexander was left but he didn't come in.

"Where do I sit?" he asked tugging at the sleeves of his agbada. I had never imagined him in one only suits like the one in his old photograph.

"Come next to Imotenya," said Mama as if it was the most obvious thing in the world.

"I thought he would sit in the back," I blurted out immediately, and I immediately regretted it. Alexander gave me a look that could murder lions. Mama smacked my arm with her hand that had a ring on it leaving a feint mark, and Aisha just grumbled something about how we were already running late.

Alexander slid in making sure to leave a more than decent space between us. Same went for me. So we were all silent as the palace gates were opened and the patrol on motorbikes went out first. There were four in front and four behind as protection.

"Your Majesty," said David leaning forward in his seat. "Can I not convince you to close the hatch."

"Don't be ridiculous," Mama snapped. It was ridiculous to think that this parade would boost the people's morale at the cost of our own. "Captain Mazarron has assured me that we will be quite all right."

"I think he's right," said Alexander looking at us with a disgruntled air. "Or better yet, don't let Imotenya come at all."

"Why, so you can parade about like some fool in my place?" I asked, glaring at him.

"I just thought you'd like to be safe, that's all," he grumbled, turning to look out the side of the car.

"Oh, and you're so concerned about my safety, are you?"

Before either of us could get in another word out we were met with flashes of light and loud cheers along the road.

Now wasn't the time to be having disputes. Now we had to put on our happy yet grieving family masks. When we got home, we could kill each other.

The roads were blocked and sections of the market were closed. Tons of people lined the streets waving our national flag and cheering. Mama waved and nudged me to do the same. I was the reason we were having this parade anyway. I pulled a smile that I'm sure if I saw it, looked unnatural and fake. I mimicked Mama's pattern of waving so that we were in perfect sync. I turned back to look at Alexander who just gave weak looking salutes to no-one in particular. I was able to feel a little better knowing he was hating this as much as I did. There was something that made this parade a less-enjoyable experience. It was after a death. If I was in the crowd, I'd be more disappointed about a well-beloved monarch than some obscure heir that just showed up here. I couldn't think about that now, my job was to be the image of a princess. To inspire hope and courage. To smile and wave.

As we passed through the Mami Wata statue and the National Museum, I saw that the crowds were thicker and louder. We were entering Ring Road, the main hub of the capital when I saw that some people were carrying placards and yelling things. I saw some of the signs saying things like 'End the monarchy', 'End corruption', 'No to oppression'. The yells I was hearing were cries of outrage at us. The words on one sign hit me hard: 'Oppressive system built on secrets'. Secrets. Before anything else could come to my head something hit off the side of the car. I heard a scream come from Aisha as a tomato splat on the side of my mother's dress. David pushed me down to the floor of the car and held me there. Alexander and Mama pressed against the sides of the car. Gunshots rang through the air and screams followed soon after as more spoilt fruit rained into the car. I thought someone had brought a gun, but then I saw it was the guards who were firing at the crowd. I pushed myself up by my elbows.

"Stop. Stop shooting!" I cried. David pulled me back down and tightened his grip on my shoulder.

We reversed quickly almost hitting the black vehicle behind as we drove back to the palace.

"For God's sake!" I heard David shout, "Put on the top!" There was a wheeze and the car's top was on, but now I could see remains of oranges, tomatoes and eggs smeared over the window. "Stay down," said David, quieter now I noticed his hand was at a gun on his belt while the other held me in my position.

We sped the way we came to the noise of screams and more gunshots and even as we hurtled through the palace gates and they slammed shut behind us, I could still hear the vicious screams, see the angry faces and feel orange juice slipping down my back. Mama, Aisha and Alexander stumbled out and were directed back inside the living quarters. I felt David pick me up slowly holding me firmly against him as we got out of the car, trying and failing to slow my breathing. I stifled a sob that came up in my throat as David and I ran up the stairs to my bedroom, startling Hanna, Petal and Miracle, placing me in Hanna's grasp.

"Get the doctor now," he said. Petal and Miracle both went out while Hanna pulled me into the bathroom. She striped me down to my underwear, leaving my dress in a pool on the ground.

"Get in the bath," she said hurriedly, grabbing a sponge. I did exactly as he said. She scrubbed hard with the hay sponge as if trying to clean the emotional dirt as well. I didn't flinch when cold water splashed on my back. She dried me off and helped me into a house-coat before leading me back into my bedroom. I wish I had stayed in the bathroom.

My mother was there in a similar house-coat along with Aisha and the doctor. The doctor came over immediately but David beat him to it and tried to lead me to my bed.

"David, stop coddling me!" I said pushing his shoulders away. I stumbled to my bed and almost fell down twice. It was only two meters away. I climbed in as the doctor drew out his flash-light and looked into my eyes.

"No signs of concussions," he muttered checking my other eye.

"She didn't faint," said Mama anxiously.

He took my pulse then shook his head. "You look fine," he said. "If a little peaky from the shock of it all."

Again, it was a shock to that effect he advised rest and little excitement. That meant he asked Aisha with her blubbering to leave the room.

On the outside I was fine, but on the inside something in me had faltered. It didn't leave with the doctor or Mama who had hugged me until my shoulders tensed or when David stepped out or when my maids came back in with tea but rather it broke and I began to cry.

Hanna came over and gave me a hug. "Oh, my dear girl," she said stroking my hair. "It's going to be alright."

I really didn't believe her. This wasn't a bunch of radicals who wanted some sort of revolution, this was the citizens turning against us. They were angry and they hated us. How long had this been going on? I remembered the amount of problems I had seen in Mama's papers. Not just roads but reports of shortages. I had never heard anything about this in Sapele provided that everything that I had access to was censored and 'need-to-know'. Newspapers were hidden from me and I couldn't watch the news. Everything they thought I needed to know was sent in weekly reports.

When was the last time a simple parade turned violent? I had the feeling never and a dark feeling came over me as if this was all my fault.

I sipped my tea almost scalding my tongue when the door opened and David came in looking as if he'd been put through a wringer. His eyes were red and he was trying not to slouch.

"Uhm, could you leave us," I said to my maids. Miracle and Petal got up immediately but Hanna was a little more hesitant.

"I'm okay," I said, giving her a weepy smile. She kissed my forehead. Before leaving with the girls.

David opened his mouth to say something, but I stopped him. "Please don't ask me how I am."

He closed his mouth and frowned. "I wasn't going to."

I put my cup on the bedside table and leaned back. "So what were you going to say?"

"That I'm glad to see you're all right."

I let out a breathy laugh. "Of course, I was, you were there and it was only food."

He came closer to my bed and knelt at the side as I remembered the noise of gunshots.

"Did you really have to shoot at them?" I asked fiddling with a loose thread on my sheets. "They didn't do much harm."

"Really?"

I might have come out with no scratches, but David saw the tear stains on my cheeks and I swear he could see the scratches on my soul.

"It was just a few warning shots," he continued drawing a hand across his lip. "I doubt anyone was hurt."

If anyone was, I don't know what I'd do. It would have been too much.

"People are just trying to let off some steam because of the king's death. It's a time of change and they want to make a statement."

I rolled my eyes. "What? That we are liars and tyrants? What would we have to lie about anyway?"

My guard didn't reply, but looked at a point on the ground, an action that seemed painful.

I licked my lips and looked around my room and compared it with what I saw on the street. It was true that many people didn't have as much as they needed in the nation but I couldn't believe that my father didn't do the best that he could for his people. It just didn't sound like him, but then again, I didn't really know him.

"I really want to do a good job," I said finally. It might not have been what I wanted for my life but it was what I was born for. "I don't want the people to hate me."

"They don't hate you. They don't know you."

I looked at David as if I was seeing him for the first time.

It was like the first time. A little girl being sent away from home, a young man being sent on an assignment. We were back where we had started and things were still the same. He could move on, advance, get away from this place if he wanted to, not be bothered with me. Ten years was a lot of time to have given your life up for someone. Then I realised I didn't want to lose him. To lose this, whatever it was between us. More than wanting to prove I could be a good ruler, I wanted to show him, he didn't waste his life by my side. "I want to prove that I'm worth protecting," I said without thinking. David's eyes softened but not to the point that they looked pitting.

He gingerly placed a hand on mine. "You are."

"There are many that can take the throne." One candidate was under this roof. "There'll never be one like you and that's why you're worth protecting."

I wished I hadn't said anything then he wouldn't have had to say anything and I wouldn't have had this feeling that I was afraid would come on me. I hadn't acted to hinder it but I never expected it to grow.

The door opened and my maids rushed back in. Miracle filled my cup and Petal turned off the ceiling fan for fear I was cold. Hanna came up to David who had since gotten up and gave him a hard look.

"Officer, the princess was told to rest," she said hands on her hips. Even though David was at least a head taller than her, he seemed to cower. "She doesn't need guards bombarding like a hurricane."

I wanted to laugh but I thought it would be ill-timed.

"I understand madam," replied David but his eyes on me now. I couldn't mistake the feeling anymore. I couldn't deny it any longer.

"Your Highness, rest well," he said with a bow and he turned and left the room.

The scratches on my soul were still there but the warm tea — now I understood why Uncle drank it — cake and constant attention covered them, not healed, covered but not as much as what I realised that afternoon. It wasn't years in the making. It wasn't inevitable but it was there all along. I was falling in love with my guard.

Chapter 19

There were no casualties at the parade, but it was all anyone could talk of. Well at least among the staff, my family didn't say anything about it afterwards, but I could still see the effects it left. Mama kept giving me tender looks and hugged me more. Alexander looked a little afraid more than sullen and had taken to eating with us again but he still didn't talk to me, even when Uncle had made a steady recovery and was actually seen around the palace. I'd heard talk of him going back to Lagos and that he'd be back in time for the burial. Of course after he had been to the Royal Records Office for what I still didn't know.

They were leaving in two days and I was walking to Mama's room after an afternoon stroll.

It wasn't as if I was outside the palace walls but I still jumped at any sudden noise. I shook my head. At least people knew what I looked like, that was a start. As I turned to a corner, I was met with the sight of Alexander coming down the stairs with a book in his hand. I braced myself — it was now or never.

"Good afternoon," I said. The name 'Best' was at the tip of my tongue. He shook then straightened and walked towards me.

"Afternoon," he said with a hint of ice. "You look well."

"Thank you, so does the Prince," I said. He nodded solemnly and moved away before I caught his arm.

"Look, I know the past week has not been easy on any of us but we must try to not to let power and control come between us. We are family after all."

He looked at me as if I was a stuffed animal for display. "I'm sorry you feel like that, but you don't know what I know."

He pulled away and lengthened his strides back down the corridor. I almost had to sprint to keep up with him.

"Tell me what you know," I said panting. He didn't turn around. He wasn't going to get away that easily. "Tell me what you know, Best."

He stopped as a guard came down the corridor and we stood against the wall as he went past. I turned to Alexander and scowled.

"You can deny it, but I know. Your sister, Patience."

He looked down at his freshly polished shoes. I didn't know how to feel exactly at that moment. Here in front of me was the pen-friend who made me like a regular girl and also the son of my rival who was making accusations against my mother.

Alexander finally met my eyes with a withering look.

"I used to write letters to you when we were kids so what?" he said, clutching the book harder in his hand.

I lowered my voice. "I was sent away so your father wouldn't be able to hurt me and I here find that his son knew where I was."

"Well, maybe your mother wasn't as concerned with your safety as you think." I was taken aback. He was really mistaken.

"Why would you be left in David's charge and not someone more experienced. It's a miracle you're still alive."

He sneered looking over me. "I'm also starting to wonder if he's messed you up. I know lots of stories of common house boys."

My chest and fists clenched and I didn't realise until Alexander was holding his nose, the book discarded on the floor, and my right hand raised, that I had hit him.

"Don't you dare talk about David like that!" I hissed. I moved to punch him again, but he quickly grabbed my arm. "You're nothing but a jealous pig."

I twisted my arm out of his grasp as he went back to nursing his nose.

"And by the way, I'm not messed up! I don't go around accusing people of things when there's no proof."

I turned on my heel and stormed down the corridor leaving Alexander, who was grunting in pain. "You know the people were right about all the secrets."

Damn him. I kept walking.

It took a few minutes before it took the pain to register on my knuckles, but eventually it did. I was too proud to go down to the medical wing. I didn't want to give Alexander the satisfaction of seeing me hurt and worst of all run into him.

I didn't hit as hard as I could have, but I did so some damage. I could see it on his face. I could have been pleased at that, but I was still hurt about what he had said. What he said about David was disgusting. If he felt the way I felt about him, people would consider that obscene as well. Then there was the issue about my mother. Why did she send me away?

Then the thought of Alexander sending me those letters. If his father had intercepted them, he could have found out where I was and then what would have happened? Would he have staged an accident like the fire that almost killed me?

I stopped walking when I had realised, I had walked past Mama's room. I groaned and edged back until I was inside the room.

"Imotenya?" 'Mama's voice called out.

"Yes," I replied, walking to her desk. She sat there hard at work preparing for a meeting later in the week. I admired her strength. Perhaps I underestimated her. She didn't have to resort to punching someone to make a point.

I walked towards her and sat in the chair at her right hand. She wordlessly handed a stack of papers for me to stamp.

She looks down at my hand in shock. "Imotenya what happened to your hand?"

I looked down at it. It was starting to swell a little. I really needed to learn how to throw a proper punch.

"I punched a wall," I said. Mama raised an eyebrow.

"Why would you do something so stupid?"

I shrugged and tried to stamp with my left hand. I was lucky to be ambidextrous, but Mama took the stamp out of my hand.

"You should get that seen to."

"I'm fine. If it's serious I'll go later."

I took the stamp back nonchalantly and stamped a letter regarding road-works. I turned to see Mama looking at me with a wistful glance.

"You're so much like your father, you know," she whispered, taking my hand. "I don't remember him ever taking vitamins. "There was a time man lived without medicine";

he'd say, and that if he wasn't dying, he didn't need a doctor."

Tears formed at the corner of her eyes and mine.

"Is that why he didn't know about his heart condition?" I asked.

She nodded, taking out a handkerchief from her dress pocket and dabbed at her eyes. I immediately regretted bringing that up as I'd regretted many things today.

She sighed. "He was so focused on his work that he usually forgot about himself." It must have been the reason he only had one wife or he was a modern man.

"He was so concentrated on his own reign, that he didn't really think of who would succeed him since he had no son."

"Is that why you pressured him for the law change?" I asked. "So I would be the heir."

"So many people were against it but I believed it wasn't fair that you shouldn't have what was your right just because you were born a girl."

I smiled at that. My mother might not have been raised a princess but she did a good job as queen by my father's side. She was able to stand up for what she believed in. But to the point of murder? No. I refused to believe she would stoop so low. If Alexander thought that David had somehow abused me, there was no point trusting anything that came out of his mouth. I was glad that he was finally leaving.

"I just hope that you made the right decision," I said. "I mean I wished I had more time to learn at his side." My throat was thick and my nose was heavy as Mama pulled me to her side for a hug.

"I know, so do I."

We sat like that for a few more minutes and even huddled

closer until Mama's necklace was almost tangled in my hair. We laughed as we pulled it out and I noticed it was a bronze chain with gold sparrow along with a straight bead at the back of her neck.

So this is what having a mother was like. A perfect blend of tough and tender.

After about an hour later when we had finished, I went down to the kitchen. I followed the smell of spice and smoke and the sound of dying chickens.

The kitchens led to a huge courtyard outside where livestock was kept and herbs were grown. Even with wealth at your disposal, natural is always the way to go. As I came in the cooks and maids bowed. I nodded at each of them as I moved to the back of the kitchen. I didn't know why I was even here. It was the few place in the palace I hadn't been to yet but I didn't understand why. The kitchen had always been my favourite part of any place.

James was there coming back from what seemed like the laundry room. He wiped his forehead with a tattered handkerchief and wiped his hands on his khaki trousers. He saw me and smiled. I smiled and too and moved towards him moving past a woman pounding yam trying to avoid the flying pieces.

"Working, are we?" I asked leaning forward against a table.

"What else?" he said, placing his handkerchief in his pocket, "Good afternoon, Your Highness."

I wanted to remind him to call me 'Aria' but then I remembered my surroundings. I didn't want anyone to think me too informal, especially since I was in the kitchen.

"I had to wash some clothes for the prince," he said, moving away from the laundry room entrance. "You know before he has to…"

"To leave?" I added. I felt sad all of a sudden. I realised that when Uncle Lucky and Alexander left, James would too. He seemed so nice and had helped me when I had asked. I didn't know him that well but I knew for a fact that I would miss him.

"Yes," he replied looking a little sombre but then he smiled. "Another change in life."

"Always comes at the least opportune time," I said with a bitter smile.

"Don't you know it."

A woman's voice called out from a bench speaking in a language I didn't understand but it sounded like a southern language.

James replied in the same language and smiled then turned to me seeing my confusion.

"She needs me to help her with some baking," he walked over and I followed him. The woman was standing in front of a mixing bowl that she filled with flour, eggs and oil. I had seen that mixture so many times.

"You're making buns," I said. The woman smiled and said something in Edo as she took some of the mixture in her hands and made a ball.

James washed his hands and wiped them on a cloth then came back and copied the woman's actions. It brought a whole cascade of memories. Saturday mornings in the sunlight with a metal bowl and bun mixture in Sapele.

"Do you want to help?" James asked, gesturing to the

bowl.

I had some work to do, but when would be the next I would do something like this with someone who may be a friend?

"Sure," I said, moving to wash my hands at the sink. James asked the cook if I could help at least that what I think he said. She replied in what I thought was the affirmative. When I went towards the bench, she stopped me and she took out a red cloth and wrapped it around my waist. An apron.

I thanked her and she smiled going back to the bowl. She took a part of the mixture and her hands worked with dexterity, and made buns in half the minute than me and James.

We placed the balls in a pan in rows. James and the cook laughed and jested. I couldn't hear what they said but it sounded happy and casual.

"She says it's not every day a princess comes into the kitchen," said James. "It means you're quite talented."

I lowered my head. "I'm not that talented, I just like to cook. I did it all the time in Sapele." He nodded rolling another ball. "It was like a family activity."

Family. They were family but not part of my nuclear family. In moments like these they felt more like my family than those surrounding me.

"My mother used to make them when I was kid," said James. "Me and my brother tried to help her, but we usually ended up licking the batter."

I giggled at the image of two boys sneaking licks while their mother's back was turned.

"Well I was never as misbehaved," I said sniffing the air haughtily. I was met with the smell of burnt goat.

"I can't believe that I hope you don't mind me saying," he replied, then looked down, arranging the balls on a pan.

"Oh really?" I said with mock offence and a hand on my hip. It left a dusty handprint on my dress.

"Well, what do you call a person who runs away from their guards and punches a cousin in the nose?"

I froze a little remembering the conversation that had led up to that but remembering where I was, I chuckled.

"I did, didn't I?"

James' eyes widened then he slowly smiled. This must have been some sort of treason on his part but we both didn't care.

Once we finished with the bowl, the cook placed a pan with oil on the fire. She tossed in some salt after a few minutes until the oil sizzled. I stepped back wary of the slashes of hot oil.

We took turns placing the balls of dough into the oil. They bubbled and squeaked and turned brown as the cook took a spatula turning them over.

"Did he tell you?" I asked James as we sat down at the bench drinking blackcurrant juice that one of the maids had gotten for us. When she gave him his glass, she looked cheerful and kept staring at him from head to toe appreciatively before she went back to washing plates.

I understood why though. Now looking at James with his grey shirt, his shy eyes and his messy hair, there was a certain charm about him, unassuming. I had always been taught about the importance of good posture, confidence and an unflinching look everything a person in my position should have. Everything James didn't have and yet he was attractive.

"That I hit him."

"He didn't," said James sipping his juice. "I figured that out myself. His nose was swollen and his father had been in his room all morning so…"

I nodded, taking a sip of my own drink.

The cook took out the buns to drain then returned to the back of the kitchen to order around some maids. "And your hand looks sore," he said pointing to my hand. I tucked it away sheepishly under a desk. It was blazing red and surged with pain when I accidently hit it off the table.

"That's what I regret the most about it," I grumbled.

James placed a hand on his cheek. "Why did you do it?" he asked then flinched. "I'm sorry; it's none of my concern."

I shrugged. "I don't see why not. He said some things. Stupid things."

"Like what you were asking me about."

"Something along those lines."

I slumped and kicked my feet that dangled from the edge of my seat. "He said some awful things about my guard, David."

"What kind of things?"

"Horrible things like how he wasn't a good guard and that he did…"

I made an uncertain gesture with my hands. James' eyes widened and he leaned in. "He thought that David did that to you."

I nodded. "A whole load of nonsense really and he also said something about my family keeping secrets."

I paused. Why was I telling him all this? It was nice to have somebody to talk to, but after the Best/Alexander issue, I was starting to get a little wary. But James was so easy to talk to.

"I'm sure everyone deserves their secrets, especially those in the public eye."

"Why are you like this?"

"Like what?"

"I don't know, good. You work for Prince Lucky's household. Wouldn't that wear off on a person?"

"Has it worn on you?"

I thought about the last couple of days. The attack had left my uncle confined, but I did receive a good bearing of his character. More importantly, I was beginning to understand why there were those who thought that he should be king. He knew things about the kingdom and was shrewd and charismatic. He, like his brother, was raised to be a ruler. And he was a male so he wouldn't break tradition. But underneath that charm I sensed something was not right about him, but then I remembered I was instilled with an inherent distrust of him my entire life and yet we had to put aside those feelings for the last week due to appearances. Maybe that's what James did.

"Not yet but I fear it will."

Before he could reply we were met with a plate of buns placed there by the cook. It was going to ruin my dinner, but I couldn't help but dig in.

"Oyese," James said to the cook. "Thank you."

"Oyses," I repeated after him recalling that basic phrase.

The cook just smiled then took my hand and said, "Ohe'Imotenya," before letting go and going back to whatever needed attending. I knew what the phrase meant. It was the proclamation that was made when I was declared the heir. 'Hail Imotenya'.

I leaned forward on my elbows taking a bite out the fluffy bun. James took bites out of his matching my position brushing his shoulder against mine causing a jolt of heat to course through me. This was so nice, it felt like what normal people did. They worked and then enjoyed the fruit of their labour with their loved ones. At least that is the way it was supposed to be if you weren't in charge of billions of people's lives.

Then a coolness came over as James got up and wiped his hands on his trousers. I immediately missed the warmth of his shoulder. Then I realised that in a few days he wouldn't be here anymore. He had been a good friend and even though I had only known him for a very short time he had managed to keep me sane in this place. What would happen now?

I got up as well and smiled at the cook who was still overseeing dinner. That's why the meals were so exquisite. A real Beni woman was in charge. I followed James out of the kitchen and back into the corridor. I bounced alongside him.

"Where are we going?" I asked.

"Well I'm going back to the Prince's room to sort out the rest of his belongings."

"Oh," I said deflated. I'm not sure I could come up with a good enough excuse to be in there especially now.

James checked the halls to see if anyone could hear us. "If it matters that much to you, we could meet up at the library." Then he ducked his head as if he had said too much. I'm sure with my uncle and cousin, there wasn't that much he could talk about. I liked to think that he wanted to talk to me as much as I did.

It mattered that much to me. "Sure, we'll do that."

Chapter 20

I resisted licking the bowl of ogbono soup and avoided looking at Alexander's swollen nose and Uncle Lucky's shifty eyes. I was in a rush to finish dinner and do whatever I had to do so I could meet James after his day of work.

"What's wrong with your nose, Alexander?" Mama asked, pointing across the table to where he was seated. An uncomfortable silence filled the air. I still didn't know if my uncle knew what happened. He just grunted and took a gulp of water.

"Nothing," Alexander muttered. "I just fell down the stairs."

Mama looked shocked. "Did you go to the medical wing?" she asked, inching forward. Alexander shook his head. "No, I sorted it out myself."

He shot me a hard glare.

"I read about a case in the government papers. A girl was molested by her family's houseboy," said my uncle casually. "What is this world coming to?"

The most random thing to any other person but I knew what it meant. Alexander had told him. "The poor girl couldn't bring herself to testify against him. It appeared to have been going on for a long time. Really messed up with her head."

I clenched the edge of the table. I knew what he was trying to do. If I was still alive, he tried to undermine my mental capability for this job. But he was wrong. Unbelievably wrong. But my mother seemed to hang on his every word.

When we left the dining room, Mama pulled me aside. Her hands were on my arms, her eyes tense and worried.

"Imotenya," she began. I didn't want to hear this. Not right now. "I want you to tell me exactly what happened in Sapele.

"Nothing," I replied. My fists clenched by my side and at the same time Mama's hands tightened on my shoulders. Why did she believe anything that Uncle Lucky had said? How could she let him stay in her house?

"Tell me the truth Imotenya."

I pulled back from her, my steps shuddering.

"Why? To make you feel better about not coming to see me all those years. You want to punish the people that actually took care of me to make you feel better about everything you didn't do!"

Two words into that sentence, I should have been slapped or thrown on the ground and beaten. But Mama didn't move. She just stood there, her eyes blank. I didn't know what to do.

My breaths came out in short bursts and before I could take another breath, Mama came over in two strides and pulled at my ear. She twisted it forcefully and I was afraid that it would fall off. "Go. To. Your. Room. Now!" she screamed. She pushed me away causing me to lose balance and fall back against the stairs. A step dug into my back and I scrambled up to my feet. Then I turned back up the stairs and didn't look back.

I held myself in a huddle on the floor of my room. I reached out tentatively to my ear. It stung. I was more than glad that my room was empty. God forbid, that I'd have to explain what happened to my maids. It was horrible. The worst thing about living with my mother was that I could be punished by her. Sure in Sapele, I had my fair share of discipline, but that was all a long time ago. I got up to get my box of letters. It was always a source of comfort wherever I was.

Before I could get to the actual letters, I stopped on the note I had found left in my room. I still hadn't handed it to David or anyone for that matter. I knew I was technically withholding evidence but I couldn't bring myself to. Perhaps if they couldn't get any further with the case I would.

I tucked the note back into the tin and pulled out the pieces of the letter Mama tore. The name Mariad Okode, Royal Record Keeper swirling around my head. Uncle still hadn't been to see him. Maybe he'd see him tomorrow before he left until further notice. Did what he wanted have something to do with Mama had asked the record keeper? It would be doubtful but at least now, I knew something more than what I had found out in the library...

The library! I was supposed to go meet James. It came at a good time too, I needed a distraction. Ignoring the fact that I had already put on my sleeping clothes, I stepped into the hallway. The guards walking by didn't say anything. They probably just thought that I was on my way to Mama's room. How wrong they were.

I passed Mama's room and would have scurried past had I not heard voices coming from the room. The door was open slightly and the voices seemed to have been coming from

Mama's sitting room.

"I did not tell anyone." Uncle Lucky's voice.

"Well keep it that way!" Mama snapped.

"If this is done right, we can appease the people and end these attacks."

My eyes widened. If there was a way the attacks could have been stopped, why had it only come now? And why was Mama discussing it with Uncle Lucky of all people? He wasn't part of any decision-making process in this country. Were they alone in there? I heard footsteps coming closer to the door and I broke into a sprint down the hall leading to the staircase.

How long has Mama been in confidence with my uncle? For a man whom she claimed was trying to kill me, she and him were awfully close. At that moment, I believed that what Mama had asked the Record Keeper and what Uncle Lucky needs from him are one hundred percent related.

James came to the library exactly sixteen minutes later. He checked to see if someone had followed him before sliding into the library.

"What, did you steal some buns or something?" I asked from the back of the library.

He jumped then turned to see me standing there with a huge grin on my face. It was refreshing, I felt I had little to smile about this whole day. Well, except the time I had spent some time in the kitchen with James. That was wonderful.

"I would have but I didn't want to keep you waiting," he said with a smile coming towards me. I smiled too. He seemed too good for this world and more importantly too good to be Uncle Lucky's servant.

He stood there looking a little self-conscious. Maybe he was supposed to be on call if my cousin or uncle needed him.

I sat back down to make him feel more at ease. He sat down opposite me.

"So how have you been?" he says leaning forward. "Sorry, I'm not used to talking to princesses."

"Well, I'm not used to talking to valets," I said. Then I grimaced. That sounded so shallow. "I meant I haven't met many valets." This was getting better and better.

"Really?" asked James, cocking his head to the side. "I thought that wherever you were, you were being taken care of."

"I was. Not pampered or spoilt but life was good." A small smile played on my lips. "Very good."

"Did your parents ever visit you?"

The smile disappeared.

"No, they didn't." I lowered my head and stared at my hands. "They always said they would but they never got around to."

James's brow was furrowed. "For how long?" I gulped. "Ten years."

As much as I didn't want to think about it, I couldn't help but hear a chant at the back of my head. "Ten years could spend a day, an hour, a minute for their own child. Their heir." For all they knew Judith could have been forging my letters, Winter mimicking my voice. But they didn't care to know.

"They must have a lot on their plate. Running a kingdom."

"Attacks have increased and the people are riled up," I snapped. "Whatever they were 'busy' doing, it hasn't seemed to work." My breaths came out in sharp staccato. I leaned back in my chair to get my bearings. "I never knew things had

163

gotten this bad."

James didn't say anything and I was wondering if he was regretting his decision in coming here.

"When you're queen, you can change things," he said eventually with a certainty that at this point I found a little annoying. This thing going around that because I was a girl, I was some sort of Messiah that was going to solve all our problems. Why me? I was only fifteen!

"Well, I hope the country doesn't fall apart completely by then."

He didn't agree or disagree with me, but looked out towards the windows at the back of the library.

The heavy curtains had been pulled back revealing a large space that ended with what seemed like the palace walls. The sky was settling to a light purplish hue with tints of brightness in the east.

"I hope you don't mind my asking but when will you be queen?" James asked, rubbing at his ankle.

"I..." I stopped. From what I had learnt, a boy became king when his father died or in some cases the father would step down and let his son rule. They'd have to be at least eighteen. "I don't really know exactly. I'll have to be at least eighteen before I can inherit."

"What if, God forbid-the queen died."

I thought about that for a minute. Even after what happened today it was awful to consider. "And you haven't turned eighteen yet," he added.

"I suppose I'll be given the title Crown Princess and rule with the help of the council." I shuddered a little at that. I hadn't met most of the advisors but with the reaction I had received from the chiefs, I wasn't sure they'd take too kindly to me.

"So you won't rule alone then," he said with a smile. "It would be hard if you had no one to go through this with."

"Yes, because middle-aged men and women make such good companions."

"It works with David." I froze.

"David is not middle aged. He's twenty-five."

"I'm sorry. It's just he is quite older than you." I clenched and unclenched my fists. Of course, he'd have his own opinion on this issue. If my uncle and cousin had discussed this, James was bound to have heard sooner or later.

"He is my friend. My best friend. He is like a brother to me. We aren't doing anything wrong." I didn't know I was gripping the chair, until I felt wood shafts seep into my fingernails. I let go of it immediately.

"I'm sorry," James said a little too quickly for my liking.

"It's fine, it's just…" I placed my head in between my legs and sighed. Then I got an idea. I came up slowly.

"James, you know the way my uncle is leaving next tomorrow."

"Yes?"

"Well, do you if he's going anywhere tomorrow to see anyone? Anyone at all?"

"He didn't mention anything to me."

I slumped.

"Why do you ask?"

"No reason."

"He hasn't left the palace walls in the last couple of days, has he?"

"No, he was recovering." I felt stung as if he was accusing

me of something. Or more specifically my mother.

"Well, I suppose it is better that he goes home, you know, to completely finish his healing."

"Will he ever?"

My eyes snapped to his, but then I understood. I had felt the same way on the same day when the palace had been infiltrated and the bombing occurred. Would I ever be free of that uncertainty, something that had been with me since I was young? And if my uncle had even an inkling of a doubt about my mother's motivations, I guess it would take even more time to completely heal from it.

"I'm really sorry about what truly happened."

"Well at least no one was killed. Hurt, but they survived."

I didn't think about anyone else who was involved. I began to feel guilty. How could I be a good ruler if I didn't know about those in my household — I tried to push that feeling away. I was kept in my room and no one told me anything, I wasn't at fault there.

"How many?" I asked, trying to still the quaking of my voice. "How many were injured?"

"About five, some pieces got inserted in a woman's leg and I don't think she's back yet. The others had some cuts and bruises. I'm sure they'll be all right."

I didn't want to imagine that Mama had been responsible for something like that. I picked at the hem of my shirt and crossed my legs.

James touched my hand gently and said, "Hey, don't think about it too much, it's in the past."

I sighed, "You make it sound so simple."

"I'm sure it's easy when you only have to worry about

sending money home to your mom." That's why he needed the job.

"What about your brother?"

James looked away from me and drew a hand across his mouth. "My brother died a couple of years ago abroad."

"Oh, I'm sorry."

He just nodded. I didn't have any sisters, but Judith and Winter were so close to me that it felt like they were. I'd be crushed if anything happened to them.

"It's strange, people think when they leave their country, they are going to a land of opportunity. They don't know that there are a whole set of problems to face."

I leaned back into my chair. "You sound as if you got that from experience."

"Yes," he said looking at his hands. "My family moved to England when I was little. It was so hard. My brother, Amos, got into some things to try and make quick money." He stared down harder and I swore I heard him gulp.

"He ended up getting shot. We took the next plane back home." I can see that he's struggling not to cry.

"It wasn't worth it," he said. "It wasn't worth it at all." I had to stop tears coming from my own eyes. It was awful to think that our people were so desperate, to leave their countries and even when they came back, it was not any easier. I huffed. It was unacceptable.

Before I could offer any more condolences, James asked if anyone would be wondering where I was.

"Not really," I replied. "Mama hit me so perhaps she thinks I've gone to sulk and will come up when I'm ready."

He looked stunned at that. Maybe I shouldn't have said

anything about Mama. Our family problems were none of his concern.

"I don't want to get you in trouble," said James, moving as if to get up. "I can't get in trouble, I'm the princess."

"But you can get hit."

"Well…"

"I think we should go, let's not take our chances."

He finally got up and extended his hand for me to take. I rose reluctantly. "Technically, I'm still on duty."

"I see, thanks for coming here, really." I didn't let go of his hand and he didn't take it from me.

"No problem Aria." It had only been a few days and I knew so much about James and he about me and I was glad that in that short space of time I had managed to make a friend in the palace.

Chapter 21

I had ended up sleeping in my own room. Mama had told me to go to my room so I did. It wasn't what I had expected, being the first time I had slept in a room by myself since I was a baby. I shivered. And look at how that turned out, I almost was burnt to death. Fortunately, I woke up in a room that wasn't filled with smoke.

Petal and Miracle came in to help me get ready. This time I readily accepted their help. With what James told me about finding work and how worried Petal was about losing her job, I decided that for all of us involved, I should let them do their jobs in peace. And what a wonderful job they did.

Miracle did my hair up in two quick braids that looked simple yet elegant and Petal chose a patterned dress for me that was in a lighter shade of black if that was even possible.

"Thank you," I said, feeling light enough to twirl around. "Thank you so much."

"It was nothing, Your... Imotenya," said Miracle quickly while Petal just smiled.

I said goodbye to them and walked down and tentatively walked past Mama room, recalling what I heard there last night. Even more strange, that my uncle was in there. Maybe Mama decided she wanted to keep him really close to her. I shuddered at the thought.

When David came to bring me down for breakfast, he looked so deflated. His forehead wrinkled, and when he thought I wasn't looking, he bit his nails. "David what's wrong?" I asked him. His eyes snapped to mine.

"Oh... um, nothing."

He became too interested in the hall in front of him. "You are a horrible liar, you know that?"

He let out a tiny laugh that could move storm clouds. "That shows I'm honest then."

"No, it only shows how bad you are at hiding things."

My guard didn't reply and stared into nothingness until I pulled at his sleeve.

"Tell me," I implored, placing a hand on the top of his arm. I let it linger. He felt so strong. "It's really nothing that you should be worried about."

I sighed. "Officer Soro, I refuse to eat until you speak to me. I stopped in my tracks and leaned back against the wall crossing my arms.

"Are you serious?" David said. I nodded with conviction. He bit his lip then came over to me drawing up to his full fight.

"Do you promise to come down if I tell you?" He was so close. I could see gold flecks in his dark eyes, I could see the way his tongue gently grazed his bottom lip. Aria get a hold of yourself.

"Yes," I stuttered, moving away from the wall slowly.

"Well, the men who came into the palace have been sent to prison, you'll be glad to know." I wasn't. Not really. Now I felt that it was the least of our problems.

"They were interviewed and it appears that they are part

of a much bigger operation. I nodded. It sounded obvious and quite timely with the king's death.

"They weren't so forthcoming mind you, but they did let something slip." My eyes widened. "What?"

David ran a hand along his chin. "One said something about how everyone will know the secrets that are destroying this nation." I shivered at the word 'secrets'. The note.

I had to bring it up sooner or later.

"Has there been any development on what happened to my room?" David shook his head.

"Not really no, sorry."

"It's all right." Tell him. Tell him now. I seriously considered it but before I knew it, we're at the dining room door.

The guards outside opened the door for me. David shoved me gently inside whispering, "I'll see you later Your Highness."

I smiled even though my chest felt heavy. I swore I would tell him later. Right now, I had to deal with the last breakfast I would have with my uncle and cousin. Hopefully, for a long while.

Mama, Alexander and Uncle had already begun the meal without me. Mama acknowledged my presence with a slight nod — I had the feeling I wouldn't get an apology for what happened last night. Uncle Lucky gave a snake-like grin, while Alexander was very intrigued by his akamu. I sat down at the end of the table and grabbed an orange while a maid poured me a glass of water. We all sat there in silence like one unhappy family.

Uncle unfolded a newspaper handed to him by a nearby steward and wordlessly flipped through the pages. I'm preoccupied with spreading butter on a slice of sweet bread when I caught a glimpse of the front page.

It was the parade. It showed rioters with their spoilt fruit and their signs. The harsh words I had tried so hard to forget rushing over me once more. I looked closer. I saw the royal envoy with the car we were riding in front and centre. I saw the guards firing into the crowd with merciless resolve and in the midst of them, I stood my face furious. Not at the people slandering my family or pelting us with their wares, no, I was facing the guards. I remembered screaming at them to stop firing but here in that egg stained dress I looked as angry as any of the protestors. I wonder why out of all the images they could have used, it had to be that one.

"Alexander, you must be pleased to be going home," said Mama with a smile obviously not having taken notice of the newspaper. "And see your mother and Patience again." I could see Mama look a little uncomfortable when she mentioned Patience Sr.

Alexander's head snapped from his bowl and wiped some akamu off his chin.

"Yes, I am," my cousin said. "The long holiday is the only time I get to see them during the year." He looked a little thoughtful. Then I realised that most of Alexander's letters from a school address and his school work was what he mentioned the most in his letters.

"They will certainly be here," interrupted my uncle, taking a sip of whatever was in his cup. "For the burial next month."

"And Imotenya's birthday," added Mama; the first proper

acknowledgement she had given me this morning.

"Ah yes," Uncle replied, then drew a hand through his beard, "Pity to have those events coincide."

I clenched the side of the table. I hated when he tried to seem so considerate. His version of pity was a punch in a pretty package.

"I'm sure it will fall into place," said Mama taking a slice of bread off the pan, "When is your birthday Imotenya?"

I almost choked on my bread. Did she really not know? Mama Osa and her husband were always busy but I never recalled either Judith or Winter having to remind them of their birthdays. But running a shop and working in the mines was nothing compared to running a kingdom. Even if you didn't seem to be getting anything done apparently.

"14th of August," I replied softly. "When's the burial scheduled for?"

"Last week of the next month."

I nodded. So I'd have a considerable amount of time before I'd have to see any more family members again.

"Then, after that, they'll be other things to think of," Mama said, her face turning into a too-quick smile.

I look around the table confused. Uncle Lucky grunted behind his newspaper while Alexander burnt his lip on his tea. Mama kept smiling.

"Coronation. Yours."

I dropped my knife. Uncle put down his newspaper and Alexander burnt his lip again. "What?" I choked out suddenly. "Coronation?"

"Yes," sighed Mama serenely as if she could picture it right now when I couldn't even get on board of the idea.

173

She took in all our expressions then slammed down her cup. "It's natural, I don't know why you're looking like goats."

I opened my mouth to speak but my uncle beat me to it.

"Why the rush, she's only fourteen?!" he said grimly. Fifteen going on sixteen. I wanted to roll my eyes.

"It's not like she'll make decisions all by herself," said Mama drawing a finger on the table. "All decisions will have to be passed through the council until she comes of age."

At that my uncle visibly slumped.

"It's what the king would have wanted," she added quickly, taking a bite of her bread. All this time, Alexander had been swaying his head back and forth from my mother to his father like a lizard. All this didn't concern him. At least it didn't seem to.

"What do you hope to do in future Alexander?" Mama tried to divert the conversation. He shrugged looking at his spoon.

"I don't know. Right now, I'm studying art and design."

"Not business?"

"I dropped it."

A warm feeling came over me. His absolute loathing of business was a staple in his letters.

I looked up meeting his eyes for a second then he quickly became interested in his cup. What had happened to us in such a short space of time?

I looked out the window behind him picking quietly at my bread. "Mama?" I asked. "Is there any information on who was in my room?"

"I'm sorry my darling but there was nothing." Her expression darkened. "The guards on duty have both been reassigned for their incompetence."

Fear didn't let me ask what her definition of reassigned was. The mood returned to its placid state before Alexander began to get up.

"May I be excused?" he said but he seemed to have all intention of leaving whether or not he was granted a request.

"Of course," my mother and uncle said in unison. He all but ignored us as the stewards opened the door for him to leave. He seemed in a hurry and it was definitely not to pack. He had a servant for that.

"Imotenya," my mother said. My head snapped to her direction and I ended up putting an elbow in the buttered remains of my bread. My uncle stifled a laugh.

"I think it would be wise if we made a special broadcast. You, speaking to the nation." I choked on warm air.

"Me?"

"Yes, you," my mother replied with a hint of exasperation. What did she expect? I felt like I was receiving an overload of events here and it was only the beginning. "To let everyone see, that you're alright, and to give them something to focus on during this time."

Yes, something other than the rising unemployment rate, the potholes on the major roads and the rebel attacks. When I thought about it, I really was here to divert people's attention.

Something novel to quell their anger but after the parade, I didn't think I was doing a good job at it.

"Wonderful idea," my uncle simpered, putting down his newspaper. "Give them another introduction to their future."

"Because the first one went so badly," he omitted. It was as if he was reading my mind.

"Mama, may I be excused?" I said, suddenly wishing to

follow Alexander's example and leave without a permit.

Mama narrowed her eyes slightly but nodded. "Be in the room in thirty minutes." I bowed and left almost getting hit as the door swung shut behind me. Coincidentally, David was coming down the hall and I jogged to meet him. I didn't know everything but I knew that a princess didn't run. Then I remembered what I had sworn to myself and wished I hadn't kept such a brisk pace. The note. I had to tell him. Now.

"David," I gulped as I stopped in front of him. "I need to tell you something."

He stiffened at my tone, eyes set as if ready to attack some unknown assailant.

"What's wrong?"

I stared at the walls, then at the windows, then at my shoes. I couldn't face him. I wasn't prepared for this!

"Well, you know the day someone came into my room…" David folded his arms across his chest.

"They left something?"

My blood turned cold. "How do you know that?" I deserved to slap myself. This was not the way I had intended on telling him. I want to break it to him gently and tactfully so he'd understand why I did what I did. Instead he was looking at me as if I was some disobedient child. I believe in a sense I was.

"How did you know they left something?" I asked. It wasn't as if he was in the room before me.

"A very reliable source told me that they saw a threatening letter in your room," he said plainly. "My guess is that it was there a couple of days before."

I bit the insides of my cheeks. "And you didn't give it up."

He had no evidence I could save myself. If I wanted to but even I couldn't defend myself from my own accusations. Why didn't I just hand it to him in the first place.?

"Aria?" David said, his expression no softer. I barely glanced up at him as I nodded.

"Yes," I gulped. "They did leave something. A note."

My guard huffed in frustration throwing his hands above his head.

"Do you know how valuable that would have been to us Aria?" he said, taking a daunting step forward. "Fingerprints, scents, anything."

"I still have it," I said meeting him in the middle. "It's still in my room." I thought of how I had kept that note at the bottom of my biscuit tin with all the rest of my keepsakes and letters. How could it have been in the open for anyone to see?

"That would be very helpful, Your Highness." the title sounded bitter coming from his lips. I turned on my heel as we headed up to my room.

It was empty. Good. I didn't need any more embarrassment. I went to my desk and pulled out my biscuit tin and pulled out the note. If it was here then I really don't know how anyone could have seen it. Unless they were outright trying to find it. I shivered in the heat. I glimpsed at the letter pieces that were also in the tin.

Should I hand them over as well? If anything, they would seem to incriminate my mother for something. I thought of what Alexander said and I pushed back that thought.

I took out the note and handed it to David. He didn't take it immediately, but looked at it as if it was some idol.

"Take it," I demanded with a coldness I didn't know I possessed. "It's what you wanted isn't it?" He takes the edge of it but I don't let go.

"If your source was so reliable," I said quietly. "Why didn't they just take it and give it to you?" David bit his lip looking troubled and he gently pulled on the note creating a slight tear.

"You would notice if something was missing from your room, wouldn't you?"

"Yes." Whoever they were they mustn't have thought that the letter was that ominous enough to hand it to security.

Finally, I let go of the note. David looked at both sides of the note, taking a special interest in the stains.

"Did you wet it?"

"No, I don't think it's water though, more like oil."

He didn't answer, but was now looking at the words on the note. The words that were still imprinted on my eyelids.

"Secrets?" David looked at me with a puzzled look, placing the note in a plastic bag. I shrugged and shook my head but that didn't calm him.

"That's what one of the men said. Secrets about the royal family."

I wanted to believe that that was a coincidence, but I 'couldn't no matter how hard I tried. My blood turned cold.

David's mouth formed a line as he understood my meaning. My breaths quickened. There was no denying it. There was a rebel in the palace.

"Aria, sit down you might faint," David said worriedly guiding me to my bed. I pushed his hand away from me.

"I'll sit down if I want to," I scoffed and heaviness came over me and I began to sway. "I'll sit down now."

I went to my bed and almost missed it. David pulled me onto it and placed his hands on my shoulders. He took my hands rubbing comforting circles kneeling in front of my bed while trying to keep his own worry at bay.

"Any guards on duty?" I choked out. "Anyone, my maids, did they not see anything that day?" David's eyes took a glassy form and an almost guilty expression came upon his face. I could tell he hated this situation as much as I did.

"No Aria. It was a priority to have someone guard your room, if you weren't there. And well, some of the guards may have become complacent with the calm."

"Calm!" I screeched jumping up from my bed. "Someone could have died in any of those attacks. My uncle was unconscious for Ogun's sake!"

"I'm not sure just anyone, they would have particular targets."

I rolled my eyes. "Thank you for the lecture, it makes me feel so much better."

I pushed past my guard and paced across the floor. I pulled at the ends of my hair, harshly undoing the braids. I needed the pain.

"Who was this reliable source of yours?" I said turning to David who was now standing, looking at me like some feral animal that needed to be sedated. "Who?"

He sighed placing a hand at the back of his neck which as I saw now was developing an unnatural layer of sweat.

"Petal," he said finally. "Petal, I believe her name was."

I stopped moving and faced him with a disbelieving expression on my face.

"While she was cleaning your room, she knocked down

179

your tin and when she was putting the letters back in, she saw the note."

Come to think of it, I did notice my letters seemed a little rumpled as if they had been put back hastily.

"She was worried and told me that she thought you might be in danger."

Some of my anger distilled. It was an accident and she acted out of a sense of duty. I could respect that. But it didn't stop me from letting out a very un-princess-like snort.

"I've always been in danger." He didn't have an answer for that.

I sat on the ground, pulling at my stocking then looked at the clock. I was supposed to be meeting Mama soon to work on my address to let everyone know I was okay. At this point, I guess the better term was think. I wouldn't be safe until these rebel leaders were safe behind bars or their heads rolling off from their bodies and my father's crown securely on my head. And then what? I'd be a young ruler and I don't know if most of the chiefs would trust me and there would also be rebuilding the country after such a trying time.

Forgetting I had company, I sprawled on the ground placing a hand across my eyes.

"David, if I ran away would you come with me?" The words tumbled out of my mouth with a frightening ease. I couldn't see his expression but I felt him approach me and came to a halt at my chest.

"I would have to," he said, his voice taking a mocking tone, "It's the only way we'd both stay alive."

A laugh escaped my lips. If it had been found out that I had escaped the palace on David's watch, he would have to pay with his life. Literally.

"Where would we go?" he asked. I pursed my lips in thought. Sapele would be an option. We could go see Ma Osa and the girls again. But that would be the first place where Mama would look for us. I thought of Lagos, our industrial capital, but then remembered I never really liked it there. Too busy and crowded although there was very little chance of being found.

Then my mind drifted to outside Xavia, further north in Auja. Auja and Xavia used to be part of a larger country years ago. After many disagreements, they broke away becoming their own republic. We had a very unsteady alliance with them. We supplied them oil and they offered us free trade of the foreign goods they acquired. With the king's death, I didn't know how long that would last but it was still a place where one could easily hide out.

"Auja," I said. "We'd go to Auja and become farmers."

David laughed and I removed my hand to see his face, light and cheerful, the way I always loved seeing him.

"What kind of farmers?"

I thought about anything I had heard about Auja. It had lots of mountains, perfect for grazing cows and...

"Sheep. We'd raise sheep."

Out of the corner of my eye, I saw David roll his eyes. "Sheep give me nightmares and it would be so boring."

I giggled at his pouting lips. They looked so soft. "It wouldn't be forever. Just until we got enough money to rent a place. Then we could get real jobs."

"You've been thinking about this a lot, haven't you?" David's voice turned thoughtful and I sat up to properly meet his gaze.

"It's nonsense I know. I would never do that."

"I know," David said with a bitter smile. "But it's nice to think that you would ask me go with you if you did."

I smiled. Of course, it would be him but he didn't need to know that, not now at least.

Chapter 22

I looked over my speech for the fifteenth time. We were at the palace's studio where most of the addresses were given if not from the king's desk which would be my desk someday. I was sitting in the studio's dressing room where a young girl was doing my makeup. I squinted through the lights on the mirrors and those coming from the main studio where they were setting up for my address.

I was nervous. I'm sure I had been on television when I was younger, but I'm not sure I had something important to say. I'm not sure what I had to say was important now, but apparently it had to be said. Mama was sitting in next to me, getting her ceremonial crown placed on her head. It was one of red beads tied together with silken threads. It was beautiful. I didn't wear anything on my head as a sign of respect for my father after his death. I wore an off-black short sleeved dress with gold leaves. Honestly, I can't remember the last time I had worn an outfit that was not a version of black. I hoped I could wear something else soon enough.

"Finished Princess," the girl said, putting down her brushes. It was typical TV make-up, nothing special, so I didn't shine on screen and yet it seemed to accentuate my features. I almost didn't look like I was supposed to be in mourning, almost.

I thanked her but, before I could finish, she bowed quickly and went to the producer. Mama came behind me and placed her hands on my shoulders, looking at me in the mirror.

"Are you ready?" she asked, holding me as tightly as I was gripping the speech in my hands.

"Yes," I said. How hard could it be? It was just reading out a little note of thanks and encouragement to the people.

"Your Majesty!" a loud voice boomed from the studio coming in our direction. It was a man, well what I believed it was. He looked more like some sort of elf. He wore a gold agbada with a golden fez with beads dangling from the sides. On his feet were matching shoes that curled at the end with little bells. He looked ridiculous, but it wouldn't be timely to laugh. No matter how appropriate it was.

He came closer and stopped into a dramatic bow. I noticed that his agbada had a tail that fluttered out behind him.

"Imotenya," Mama said. "This is…"

"Goodluck, Egbe," I finished. How could I not know him? On the rare occasions we watched television in Sapele, he was a daily feature on Xavian television. The royal correspondent ever since I was born. He was entertaining but most of all he had a ridiculous wardrobe. Each daily outfit seemed worse than the other. One time he was wearing a peacock feathered hat with a swan feather shawl and he was speaking on the financial state of the country. Honestly, he belonged on the runway.

When he saw me, his mouth stood agape as he hurriedly shook my hand.

"So this is our lost princess," he said looking at me from

head to toe. People seemed to do a great deal of that at court. Eyeing you up, striping you bear, to see if you are a friend or foe. I would have to get used to this.

A smile came across my lips. "I was never lost just momentarily misplaced." That elicited a laugh from Egbe, but a sad look from Mama. I felt a little guilty.

"Are you ready, Your Highness?" he said with a chuckle.

"Yes," I said a little uneasily but we made our way into the main studio. Uncle Lucky, Alexander and even James sat in the corner on couches. Security was around as well, but they seemed a little preoccupied and I caught sight of David, his eyes scanning the perimeter analytically. Then our eyes met and a disarming smile crossed his lips. Then I turned to where my cousin and my uncle sat with James behind them. James looked around the bright studio with its gaudy decorations and settings.

Our eyes met. His eyes seemed to glisten with the artificial light and an almost homesick look came across his features. He looked so peaceful but sad. Nevertheless, he smiled shyly at me drawing a grin out of me.

Mama steered me to the cameras and I felt like the lights could burn through my skin. There were plush leather couches in front of three camera men. A studio hand placed a microphone on the back of my dress adjusting the mic towards my mouth so that I could almost taste it. Mama had hers on as quickly as possible before she sat down on the couch, a maid arranging her hair and dress around. I sat down beside her straightening my dress. Egbe came to us after having a brief conversation with my uncle. It seemed really intimate, but it was just a conversation between old friends.

He sat on the couches between Mama and I as instructions

were exchanged between the others in the studio. Cameramen went to their stations behind their cameras as the lights were adjusted to lighter glare. Another man who I thought was the executive producer came behind the camera-men and went into a countdown.

"3…"

I looked down at the cards. "2…"

I straightened up and looked at the camera. "1…"

"Good afternoon, Xavia," said my mother. Her ankles were crossed like a proper lady and her stature was that of a queen, albeit a queen in mourning.

"In the wake of the death of my husband, the King of Xavia, our nation is in a state of turmoil. The recent attacks in Enugu state have left many devastated as well as the others in recent times."

She fell silent for a bit. Then Good luck Egbe interrupted with his brand of vivacious charm. "Yet in spite of all this," he said with a smile. "There is a spot of hope." He turned to me and took my hand. "The return of our lost daughter, Princess Imotenya Aria Accra."

I gave a 1001-watt smile. I guess saying that I was a lost princess gave the story a certain sensationalism. There were people who knew exactly where I was. I glimpsed at Alexander and his father in the back. More than I would have wanted.

"Indeed," Mama said with a bright smile of her own. "I'm ecstatic that she's home." If not for protocol and Good luck Egbe sitting between us, she might have taken me in her arms then and there.

"I'm very happy to be home too," I said. Egbe gave me a

nod. This was the signal for me to begin.

"It was hard to be apart from my loved ones for so long especially with the shadow of rebellion and certain death over all our heads. My father, the King, strived tirelessly to put a stop to this plague on our land." I thought that was very strong and didn't know how true it was, but I continued. "These rebels, whatever they want, cannot be worth the lack of trust and terror that our people live in. We, the royal family, will not stand for it. Our best men are out there and will put an end to this terror once and for all."

That was it. That was all I had to say, but not all I had to say.

Before Egbe and my mother could get another word in, I went into my own unrehearsed tirade. "One more thing. This is your land and we are only caretakers. Fight," I said resolutely. "Fight against this threat any way that you can. Defend your friends and your neighbours. These people, whoever they are, don't seem to stop their fight so why should we?"

A heavy silence ensued across the studio and the executive producer gestured wildly to Egbe, signalling him to wrap things up, or at least stop looking like a gutted fish.

"W-well," he stuttered in confusion trying to get his bearings back with a huge grin on his face, but his eyes didn't seem focused. "You've heard from our lovely princess." He tightened his grip on my hand anxiously. I didn't need anyone to tell me that Mama's eyes would have the same effect. "Later on, we will present the weekly report. I'm Goodluck Egbe and good day."

The camera's stopped rolling and in the once quiet studio,

hell broke loose.

It started when Uncle Lucky strode over fists clenched at his sides. He leaned over me making a considerable effort to highlight our height difference.

"What do you think you're doing?" he seethed stopping short of grabbing my arm in the room full of people. "That wasn't what we wrote for you."

I blinked. "We?"

"I had him go over the speech for me," Mama said from behind me coming closer once she had removed her microphone from her dress. That would have been a smart thing to do.

"It's not as if I ignored it completely," I retorted. "I said everything you gave me."

"And gave a piece about telling the people to fight!" my uncle's eyes were alight with fury, the complete opposite of the cool and calculating man I had come to know over the last week.

"Or have you forgotten the incident at the parade? Those people don't need another incentive to get unruly."

I wondered if he knew that some of "those people" were surrounding us right that moment going about their business cleaning cameras and rearranging the studio, if they took notice of how he regarded them as some primal beasts.

"I was not encouraging revolt, just that they stood up for themselves against the rebels."

"Nevertheless," Mama commanded coming between us. "Next time you say only what we give you to say all right?"

She said that low enough so only I could hear it, but I felt as if the whole studio was listening in. I gulped. "Yes Mama, I will."

"Good," she replied pushing my uncle away from me and back to my cousin who looked like he was waiting for the whole story of what happened. I couldn't deal with much more of this. I untangled myself from the microphone handing it to an AA. I said a quick goodbye to Egbe, saying I needed to leave claiming a headache which he guffawed at and asked if his company was that terrible, I politely denied it before scurrying out of the studio, not even considering whether or not I had a guard with me.

I made it across the courtyard to back to the living chambers and leaned back against the shade beside the door.

That didn't go so bad. Did it? Regardless of what my uncle and my mother said, everyone else in the studio didn't look too incensed. Not that I focused on what anyone else was doing after that scolding. I sighed and closed my eyes. For something that I knew would be mine my whole life, I appeared to be very poorly prepared for it.

"Princess?"

My eyes opened and I saw David standing in front of me. I should have known no matter how fast or far I ran away, he would always follow me.

"I'm fine," I said before he could ask. I pulled at the baby hairs slowly appearing out of my braids. Before either of us could say another word, Aisha scampered over with an elderly man behind her.

"Good afternoon Your Highness," she chirped once again checking her clipboard. "I'm sorry I didn't get a chance to see your address because as you know work, work, work."

I nodded with a smile glimpsing at the man behind her. He dressed like a southern man with a black bowler hat with a green buba and black trousers. He was bald with sparse hairs at each side of his head.

He gave a slight bow as much as his cane would allow.

"Your Highness, it's an honour. Sorry about your father, he was a good man," he said, revealing two gold teeth. He reached out for my hand and I shook it nonchalantly until what came next. "I'm Mariad Okode, I'm here to see the Queen."

My hand went limp in his and wasn't until I noticed David glaring at our hands that I had the natural sense to pull away.

"The Queen will be here shortly," Aisha said, already going into the living quarters. "I'll show you into the living room."

Okode followed but then turned back to me and tilted his black bowler hat. "Princess." He gave one last grin before going inside with Aisha.

Mariad Okode. That was Mariad Okode here in the palace. Something in me leapt but then I wondered why was Mama seeing him and not Uncle Lucky? Perhaps she has to personally screen all the prince's visitors but he specifically said that he was coming to see Mama. A chill came over me. I couldn't, wouldn't believe that they were going to see him together.

There was something wrong going on here. When did this truce with my uncle start? They consorted in her room, had private discussions and now were receiving a guest. This was beyond keeping your enemies close, this was all out working with them.

Perhaps it was a moment of weakness. This was a very trying time for all of us especially Mama. Yes. She was falling right into my uncle's arms with no thought whatsoever. Good thing he and his infernal son were on their way far west tomorrow. Not a moment too soon indeed.

"Good job today," said David, clutching me from my thoughts. I turned and gave a wry smile. "If only Mama thought the same."

"I'm sure she does, maybe she felt a little pressured by the prince."

"But why would she be?" I drew the hand along the banister as we went upstairs but my eyes were fixed on the door behind which sat Mariad Okode and all he knew about whatever it was my mother and uncle were hiding.

As if on cue Mama came into the living chambers and walked into the room. Mere moments later, Uncle Lucky slipped in looking devious as ever. If only I could hear what they were saying.

"Strange man isn't he," said David, taking note of how I hadn't moved an inch in the last couple of minutes. He had no idea how strange. It pained me to think of how much I was hiding from him but I couldn't just drop all the rumours of treason, all the suspicions, all the threats on him now.

"Well, he spends all his time with books, you wouldn't expect him to be normal."

He chuckled urging me onward to my room to prepare for my lessons. They seemed less daunting after this morning's address but before I could think any more on the subject, a shout broke out from downstairs.

I charged back to the bannister over the floor and saw the living room door fling open and Mariad Okode rush out scrambling to pick up some papers that had fallen from his hands while my uncle was yelling at him, shaking his hands about.

"Don't you dare show your face back here saying such nonsense, you hear!" he bellowed before going back inside.

I raced down the stairs almost falling, while David called for me to stop. I almost ran over Aisha who was charging to the living room, probably to Mama's aid.

I turned to see a few guards surround Okode to see that he left the palace with no further incident. I caught his eye and there was a strange look in them. Almost pitying. The only one who should be sorry for themselves is him. He's got the embarrassment of being dragged out of the palace after having the idiocy to do or say whatever he said to the queen.

I ran to the doors and I didn't wait for the guards to open them but charged in to see Aisha trying to calm my mother who was pacing back and forth in front of the window while my uncle continued to curse at Okode. They turned to me with rage and uncertainty in their eyes.

"Imotenya, shouldn't you be preparing for your lessons?" she seethed trying to regain her composure.

"What did he want?" I asked, ignoring my mother, looking at my uncle. If anything, I knew he would give me some sort of answer. He was pressing his temples but before he could reply, the doors were pulled open again and Alexander stepped in, moving past David.

"What's happening?" he asked, pulling at his necktie.

"Nothing!" my uncle and Mama yelled. Whatever happened, they didn't want either of us to know about it.

"It's not nothing!" I yelled back and turned to Alexander who looked as confused as ever. "The Royal Record Keeper was here and your father threw him out and he upset my mother."

At the mention of Mariad Okode, Alexander stiffened a

little and clenched his fists. Mama took notice and looked at Aisha coldly.

"Leave us please."

Aisha bows quickly and hurries out. She left her clipboard.

"You too." I saw mother point to the wall where David was standing. He didn't flinch at her tone. He just looked at me as if asking for permission. I nodded quickly. I won't die here.

He bowed, opened the door then left with one last look at me.

None of us spoke. Mama sat down on a couch beside the window. Uncle leaned against a bookshelf. I turned to Alexander whose fists were still clenched. On closer look, I saw that he was holding something. A balled-up sheet of paper. Though ancient it looked official. Like a royal record.

Without thinking I moved towards him, tearing his hands away from the crumpled paper. I opened it up. It was a birth certificate. I looked at the name on top. It was mine.

Name: Princess Imotenya Aria Accra District: Oredo
Gender: Female
Place and date of birth: Palace of Beni. 14th of August NE104 Mother: Her Royal Highness Beartrice Ighohemena Ikha Accra
Father:

I shuddered. The paper fell from my hand. I fell forward clutching the side of a sofa. It wasn't enough. I couldn't stand so I fell into it. I didn't say anything. I couldn't.

Mama rushed over towards me trying to shake me from my stupor. I closed my eyes thinking that if I could, what I saw would clear from existence. It didn't. It played behind my eyelids that were barely holding back the tears. *Father: His Royal Highness Prince Lucky Immanuel Accra.*

Uncle Lucky.

Chapter 23

The prince picked up the now discarded birth certificate. He wanted to see what got the children into such a state. Both his children.

He didn't shout. People would hear. He didn't have the audacity to look like he didn't know what had just happened. He just kept saying one thing as he handed it to my mother, his eyes on the floor.

"Why? What use did he have to keep this? Why?"

Mama saw it and clamped a hand over her mouth. She moved to hug me but I shifted away. Alexander was on his feet, hands in his pockets glaring at his father.

"Why shouldn't he have kept it, Father?" he hissed. "Why shouldn't he have kept the truth?" The prince's head snapped up, eyes like fire baring into his son.

"Because look what the truth has done to us," he hissed gesturing to all of us, "It hasn't made anything better."

My eyes met his and for a moment his anger died as he came towards me. Like I did to Mama I recoiled from his touch. So turned back to his son.

"Where did you find that?" he asked, his voice trembling with an uncharacteristic fear. "Where was it?"

Alexander met his eyes looking hurt, but not easily

deterred. Where had the complacent boy I had met when I first arrived here?

"It was on the ground," he said flatly.

The papers that were falling out of Okode's hands. I would have laughed at the irony. Out of everything he had brought with him today, my birth certificate, my real birth certificate, had to be the one to fall in front of the stairs. But for the prince, it was no laughing matter.

He pulled at his hair and his breathing quickened. "What if someone else saw it before you did?" he said hurriedly. "What if someone else knows?"

"What would we do?" Mama said sharply, startling us all. "Get rid of every guard and maid that was on duty? Get rid of Aisha?" I could see that that prospect was not one she would consider. "Do you really think that would make things better?"

"If it was true," I whispered. My voice was weak, but somehow it managed to carry through and cause everyone to look at me. "Is it true?"

Mama and the prince looked at each other uncertainly, each begging the other to deny it.

Please deny it. Please. It's not true. My father was dead, soon to be buried.

"It's true." The prince's voice rings in my ear like a funeral bell and Alexander stifled a gasp before running out of the room slamming the door behind him.

The prince rose to go after him, but was pulled back down by my mother.

"Talk to him later," she said, her hand lingering on his arm to get him to look at her. "Imontenya needs to know."

I didn't know what else I needed to know. The man I had

196

grown to despise and distrust was my father. My father. That's why Mama was not worried about being so close to him this last week. They were something much closer in the past.

But I had so many questions but I couldn't get my lips to form any of them. Then realisation hit me.

"Mama, Baba...," I stopped. No, he wasn't that to me, "The King doesn't have an heir?"

She nodded. That meant that rule would pass to his brother's eldest child. Something cold gripped my chest.

"That means Alexander is..." None of them finished my sentence. They didn't have to. "After all this time..."

My voice broke, but the prince put his hands on my shoulders as if that gesture would make up for all the lies.

"You have to understand: no one of consequence knows, except Okode, but he can easily be dealt with." I didn't want to consider the implications of his words. I shook his hands off me and stood moving as far as I could away from them.

"You have to understand why we did it."

"Did what?" I choked struggling to keep my voice low. "Betray your brother, betray your wife, and betray the king."

"I was trying to help him," he said sharply. "If we didn't do what we did there would have a crisis."

I paused when my back hit the wall. He sighed running a hand through his beard. Mama spoke up.

"The doctors said that the king had very little chance of producing a child. They tried everything they could but it was no use." She paused and a bitter smile crossed her lips, "But he kept trying. It was driving him insane. So he asked Lucky for help in that area. That way, the child would still be in the Accra bloodline."

She turned to the prince for his confirmation. He didn't

disagree. She went on.

"He wasn't married then so he wasn't breaking any law. Then I had an heir."

"Me?" I said believing I had gotten a hold on this unbelievable story, but she shook her head. "Not you my dear," she gulped, pressing her hands together. "Alexander."

As if the shock couldn't get any worse. I thought I knew that boy. It was pitiful how little I didn't now and shocking how much I was finding out.

"After that everything was fine," the prince began taking a seat to steady himself. "The kingdom had an heir and no one was any the wiser."

I wondered if they had forged a birth certificate for Alexander like they did for me so no one suspected. But Auntie Patience must have been in on it too. I wonder what she was promised or threatened with.

"But what happened with... me?" I asked. I couldn't completely understand that part. Or maybe I did, but I still didn't want to believe it.

Mama looked to the side painfully while the prince stared at the floor. "Tell me," I said louder, clenching my fists. They owed me this.

Mama turned to me, tears shining at the corner of her eyes.

"I was exhausted and overwhelmed that Desmond told me to go have a break. I went to one of our houses in Lagos. Lucky came to visit me." She gulped. "He was alone."

She didn't need to go on.

"When I found out I was pregnant. I told Desmond it was his. That you were his." She closed her eyes letting a tear fall down her cheek, and a tiny smile graced her lips.

"Even though the dynasty was secure with Alexander, he was so happy. A child of his own." Now tears came in my eyes. How glad he must have been to discover he was going to have a child; in his case, a miracle child. I knew I shouldn't have felt that way, but I was glad he had died before any of that could come to light. At least I hoped that's what happened.

"Wait," I said, suddenly noticing something. "What about Alexander? If he was said to be the king's son, how could I have contested for the throne?"

The prince got up and placed a hand close to the edge of the sofa.

"Alex was born 10 months before you." He pulled at his hair meaning he really was uncomfortable talking about this. "We staged his death. Patience was said to be pregnant during that time. Then all of a sudden." He clicked his fingers. "She had a son, the king had a daughter, and the new law made her an heiress." He nodded towards me.

I didn't know what to say. It was such a well-kept secret: one that could lead to more problems than we had if anyone found out. But a dark feeling in the pit of my stomach told me people knew, apart from Mariad Okode and I can't imagine who else.

"But that damn Okode is threatening to ruin everything," the prince sneered with years' worth of malice in his voice.

"He says that we should bring this up before the council of chiefs," Mama said her eyes faraway. "To make a decision. Even if you're a ruler you're still under the law."

"What could they say?" I asked, anxiety pulsing through me and wasn't sure if I really wanted to know.

Mama sighed leaning back against the couch. "We went against the law and should legally be disposed of or…"

"Or?" I pressed.

The prince headed towards the window, leaning against the frame with a placid look on his face.

"Or when we tell them the truth, they uphold the law and... and make Alexander king."

There was water in my ears, or a horn was blown and I was deaf. Anything else. Anything else but this. Be disposed of, whatever that meant or Alexander be king. Alexander a boy who could hardly meet people's eyes. Alexander who loved books and wanted to be an architect.

Alexander, king? Were they mad?

And where would that leave me? My whole life I've been preparing for when I'd take the throne. That was all I knew. Without that I was nothing.

My heart was heavy and I clenched and unclenched my fists. I thought I was special that I would bring hope but now...

I bit my lip drawing blood. My life was a lie, a mistake. A mistake that could destroy us all.

I turned to my mother and all I could see was red. All I could see was the woman who broke her vows, betrayed her husband, abandoned her daughter because she couldn't stand to suffer the consequences. The woman who had lied and ruined my life.

"I can't believe you," I whispered with venom. I didn't care that tears were rolling down her cheeks and kept muttering apologies. So un-queen-like.

I rose up with the look at the man I had been raised to fear. My father. This was sickening. He didn't turn from the window. I didn't want to consider what was going through that twisted head of his. How far he would go to keep their secret.

I stormed out, struggling to breathe, not caring who saw. There were worse things in life than people seeing you cry, so much worse. I ran up the stairs to the guest chambers to the person, who like me was living a lie.

He opened before I even knocked. He looked as he did when his father-our father- had been injured, only this time the wound was not some contrived assassination attempt. It was much deeper.

In that moment I set aside our animosity and embraced him. It was a few minutes before his arms crushed against my spine.

Alexander was more intelligent than I gave him credit for. He must have known something about this. That's why he left. He understood and he didn't need it spelled out to him.

"I'm so sorry," I said. "I'm sorry."

"It's not your fault," he replied into my hair.

No matter what he said, I couldn't believe it. Despite what I said to Mama, for all her mistakes, this wouldn't have happened if I wasn't born.

We parted awkwardly and went into his room. I sat on his bed while he poured me a glass of water. On closer inspection, I saw it wasn't water, it was vodka.

I didn't care. I almost drank it in one gulp.

"Easy now," Alexander chided, pouring his own glass and refilling mine. "You don't want to go to the hospital wing, do you?"

I laughed feeling light-headed. I was still worried, still angry but I didn't feel it so much. "No, I'll be sick with all the germs and the needles, and the sickness."

I took a huge gulp. I felt so good. I didn't understand all this talk about hospitals. I felt like I could move mountains.

That was until I remembered our conversation.

"Is that what you meant Best?" I said sipping my drink again. "All the secrets?" Alexander didn't answer but leaned back against the table in thought.

"No," he said silently. "No, it was some other thing but this. This tops it all." I nodded violently, spilling a little of my drink on the Lino floor.

"People know," I muttered. "People know and what will people say?"

"I don't know but, knowing the queen, she'll have a few tricks up her sleeve."

"The queen?" I hiccupped looking at my cup. It was empty now. "Ah, the queen. Our mother." Silence. I don't think Alexander was there for that part.

He dropped his glass on the table and stalked towards me. His disinterested air gone and replaced with something sinister.

"What did you say, Teny?"

I moved back on the bed hitting the perfectly arranged pillows. "No-nothing Best."

He grabbed my wrist with hands of steel. His eyes blared. "You said the queen was our mother. Were you lying to me?"

His grip tightened and I was too drunk and out of mind to even think about shoving him off. "I..."

"Right."

He let go of me, suddenly, letting me fall back against the pillows, finally leaving them in disarray.

He stormed out of the room pushing past the guards that seemed to be stationed outside his door. Before I could even imagine what had happened, I heard my name.

"Aria?"

I turned to the door that had been left wide open and saw my guard staring at me.

I hopped off the bed, discarding the cup wherever and waddled to the door into David's arms.

"He looks angry," I said staring down the corridor. He had most likely gone downstairs to Mama and Uncle. No, Mama and Father. He will be so mad when he finds out.

I turn to David as he leads down the corridor to my room, I think.

"I don't understand why though. I feel happy. Happy, happy, happy." I swayed from side to side without a care in the world. Who cared that my hated uncle was my father? Who cared that my mother had been lying to me my whole life? And who cared that there were a bunch of people that wanted us dead? Not me.

In all this, I hadn't noticed that David had pulled me to the side and knelt in front of me. He sniffed the air in front of me. A deep frown came across his handsome features.

"Have you been drinking?" he asked suspiciously. I smiled innocently. "What in heaven's name would make you say that?"

I playfully shoved him, but he didn't budge. "Did he get you drunk?"

I think he was referring to Best.

"Oh no. He warned me to stop, but I didn't; I kept going and now I feel so good." I hopped on the spot almost reaching his shoulder.

"Why don't you look happy?" I whined. "I will have your head for not smiling."

"You need to go to your room," my guard said coming towards me, but I shrunk back. Who was he to tell me what to do? I stepped back further but somehow my right foot caught on my left foot and I was on the floor. I giggled finding the whole thing funny.

"A talk with Mama and I can't walk properly, no change there."

David sighed and called to somebody behind me, saying words like doctor, now, emergency.

I wanted to protest but I ended up on my side like a dying freshwater fish on land. Being a fish was the same as being a person. You swam happily along until you were speared in the stomach.

Luckily, I didn't feel a spear on mine, just a cool hand propping me upright and dragging me up to my feet.

"Come on... Oh. Never mind."

David picked me up barely dodging a hand to the jaw and a kick to the nose.

We were back in my room before we knew it and I was so tired that I didn't protest when David put me down on my bed.

"Sit up, sweetheart," he said trying to get my head to rest against the headboard. I just wanted to lie down.

I kicked furiously — at what, I didn't know. David placed a hand comfortingly on my shoulder. I couldn't shrug it off, nor did I want to. It felt almost as good as I felt after I had what Best had given me. But right now, I had a stomach-ache: a stomach-ache that was going to take away all my happy feelings.

I groaned and looked up at the gold encrusted border of the ceiling. We had so much but yet we still weren't free. All our money couldn't buy away the consequences of past wrongs.

Consequences that were eating me up right now.

"David?" I said eyes still fixed on the ceiling that was now becoming extremely blurry. "Do you regret working for the royal family?"

A pause.

"Not really, but sometimes… I don't know. I don't like seeing you miserable that's all."

"And you think they make me miserable?"

A longer pause that turned into silence. Wise. And as the doctor came in with his friendly manner, I believed I heard shouting coming from downstairs.

Chapter 24

I didn't suffer from any midday hangover when I woke up and the doctor despite his smiles seemed to be a little exasperated at being called for one minor ailment after another in the span of a week.

I stayed in my room alone for the remainder of the day skimming through books and picking through meals. Mama had the decency not to call on me throughout the day, not for meals not for work or anything else and if she did, I doubt I would have gone and if I had I, there was a good chance I might have broken down.

Miracle tried her best to talk to me and Petal was sweetly at my absolute beck and call, but I all but ignored them. I even told David to stand outside when he tried to understand what had gotten me so upset that I ran to my cousin of all people, and more to the point why I allowed him to get me drunk.

It pained me to the core that I couldn't tell him. Not if I wanted him to be safe. That was a secret that had been kept for fifteen years and doubted neither Mama or the prince would want it getting out anytime soon. I leaned back on the chair of my desk and my mind suddenly turned to Mariad Okode. Did he just come here to tell the queen that he knew her secret? Was he blackmailing her? And what made him catch on in the first place?

My breath caught in my chest. I wondered if Mariad Okode didn't get what he wanted, would he expose us or force us to put the rightful heir on the throne? I paused. Then what would happen to me? Would they fake my death like they did with Alexander? A sick feeling came to my stomach. What if they forwent faking all together? One small accident. A trip down the stairs, food poisoning. Death from a fire set to a nursery. No one would suspect a thing.

Tears pricked at my eyes. No, I wouldn't believe that of my mother. She had an affair and produced a child without telling her husband, who knows what she could be capable of.

I shook my head. It wasn't true.

There was a knock at my door. I rushed towards it at first then went back to check myself in the mirror. I didn't look too bad just a little flushed, that was all.

I went back to open my door and saw a maid standing there with two letters in her hands.

"I was asked to deliver these to you, Your Highness," she said with a bow. I took them from her and mumbled a thank you before going back into my room. That wasn't so bad.

I sat on my bed taking the first letter that was in an envelope. It was addressed from Sapele. I tore the envelope and pulled out two letters. I took out the first one and began to read.

To Aria,

I can't believe you're at the palace! With a staircase too, you have to slide down it if you're allowed. Tell me more about the food. Do you eat whatever you want, do you eat cake every day? I'm glad the queen is all right and I can't believe Prince Lucky is there too. I hope that you're safe and that Uncle David's taking care of you. Mummy misses having another man around the house when daddy is away. Judith is so much fun this summer. I think she misses you two.

I'm continuing with my painting and some artist came by and said that one of my pieces deserved a place in the Lagos galleries. I'm so happy. I know mummy would want me to study to be a doctor like Judith but I really want to be an artist. I hear there's a great art school in Benin. Maybe if I go there I could do paintings for the palace then we could see each other every day.

I really miss you Aria. Write again soon.

Winter

P.S Say hello to the queen for me. I'm not sure she knows who I am though.

P.S.S I wrote a letter to Uncle David. Don't read it.

I laughed and cried at the same time. Sweet Winter. What wouldn't I do to make her dreams come true. To make all their dreams come true. To make sure Judith can easily get through medical school. To make sure Ma Osa's business succeeded and to let Winter follow her passion. But it wasn't that simply. Not anymore. Not when the life and position of my immediate family was hanging in the balance.

If only I could go back to the day I first arrived. Before the insane family introductions, before the lessons and lectures when I was just a girl grieving for her father. I let out a bitter sigh. But he wasn't my father. My father was under this roof, plotting and planning as usual. I looked at the second letter and saw that it was from said father. I was tempted to tear it in pieces and say that I didn't get it but somehow common sense won though.

I looked at it. It was inviting me to his chambers with my mother. I pulled at the ends of my dress. What would he have to say now? I don't have to go though. Who would blame me but after the arguments this morning, we could at least talk civilly.

I picked up Winter's extra letter and left my room. David and the other guard turned almost as quickly as I had opened the door. I nodded to them both before pressing Winter's letter into David's hand.

"From Winter," I whispered with a smile.

I walk towards the staircase going down to my uncle's room. David trailed behind me as if the events of today hadn't happened at all.

"Where are you going?" he asked, catching up to my side.

"To my uncle's chambers," I said. The words feel bitter on my tongue.

"Are you sure that's a good idea?" my guard replied, stopping suddenly.

"He invited me. Mama will be there too."

I didn't need words to know that that reassured neither of us.

"I know you're worried, but it's nothing. He probably just wants to say goodbye before he leaves tomorrow."

David frowned and his hand shifted to his face. I could tell that he didn't believe me for a second. I'm sure he was surprised a direct attack on my life hadn't been made already. If only he knew how dire things had gotten already.

I looked at him with soft eyes. If only he knew so many things. How I wasn't the rightful heir that I believed I was.

How even if things died down and I somehow ascended the throne, I would always feel like a fraud. How he felt like the only thing that was keeping me afloat in this sinking sand of a palace. How I loved him.

I knew my duty. Marry some chief's son when I came of age and the courting season began, produce an heir all while ruling the kingdom. But none of the lessons, none of the reminders of my duty, my entire life could stop the late-night fantasies. Dreams about what my life could be like with David. They were wonderful but they also hurt because it could never be and with what I had found out today, that dream seemed further than ever.

We came to my uncle's chambers when David touched my wrist making me even dizzier than I had felt this morning.

"I'll be right outside," said David, his voice drenched in worry. I took his hand.

"I'll be fine," I said, forcing a smile. "And if I don't come out, you'll know what has happened to me."

He didn't laugh. This wasn't a laughing matter.

I walked to the prince's chambers and knocked on his door.

"Come in," his voice called out.

The guard opened the door and I stepped in.

I saw the prince and my mother sitting down in a deep conversation. I wondered if their relationship continued, after I had been born. I shuddered at the thought.

"Sit down."

I stayed standing. He sighed.

"I want you to listen very carefully," he droned as rehearsed, "Not a word about what was said can get out to anyone you hear?"

Well, obviously.

"Not your maids, not your guards, no one."

"I'll do a better job than you did."

Mama gasped at my bluntness, but the prince just stared me down. "Maybe it would be best if we got rid of all your companions."

It was my turn to gasp.

"You can't do that — they don't know a thing!"

"Oh, and you make a habit of speaking to the help?"

I wanted to punch him like I did his son. I didn't care if he was my father, he wasn't acting like one. "Forgive me for trying to associate with people of character, since I have very little of that in my own family."

"Imotenya!" Mama snapped. "You don't want me to flog you, do you?"

I shook my head and sat down opposite them, wringing my hands.

"I told you she wasn't prepared," she sighed, placing a hand to her temples. I supposed her headaches were coming back.

"I'm sorry it had to come to this," the prince. Did they not remember that I was still here? He then turned to me, eyes downcast, as if carefully choosing his words.

"Imotenya, honesty is a very important trait in every man or woman." A trait you do not seem to possess.

"A trait that could lead to the downfall or success of that man or woman. And now it seems this secret is bringing about our downfall."

I'm glad you can see that.

"But there is a solution." He turned to my mother who

seemed engrossed by the whirring of the A.C.

"We came up with a solution."

I leaned forward hitching my skirt up above my knees which were starting to get goose bumps. What had they decided?

"You are relieved of your title and duties as Crown Princess." The world stopped spinning. The room tilted. The sky fell.

"The heir is now Alexander, your cousin. It'll be announced soon enough."

I struggled to form words. "Will they know the truth?" I croaked. "The full truth?" My parents glanced at each other nervously. I could tell the answer was no.

"No," Mama replied sitting up straighter. "We will say that the princess has stepped down due to health reasons, leaving the throne to her next of kin: Alexander."

I shot up, almost knocking back the chair.

"Does Alexander know about this?" I heaved out. That A.C was making the air unbreathable. "We spoke to him earlier," Mama replied softly. "He agreed with us."

"Did he? Or did you command him?"

She didn't answer. She didn't have to command. He just needed a speech about duty, family and how we were on the verge of being overthrown, to get him to agree but that didn't mean it didn't hurt. I wasn't the heir anymore. What had my life been for?

"It's a good plan," the prince said soberly as if discussing a plan for a new piece of land he had just acquired. "The chiefs are satisfied. The throne stays in our family and no one has to be none the wiser about anything else."

My neck almost snapped as I turned to him sharply. My

eyes were stinging and my throat was closing up.

"What will happen to me?" I said.

"You will stay here obviously," replied Mama coming towards me. She placed her hand on mine with a smile. What was there to smile about? I looked at them both in turn, disgust clouding my eyes.

"Is that all you think about," I sneered. "Nobody finds out about your secret, keeping the throne in the family when you clearly don't care about the people that are under it!"

"Imotenya..."

"No, what exactly have any of you been doing for the people of this country besides plotting and scheming for things you don't deserve!"

"And what would you do?" the prince said rising up and stalking towards me. His eyes were like that of a wild beast, ready to pounce on his prey. "What do you know about ruling a kingdom? It's more than what you've read in your books. The truth is you're not ready and I'm not sure it's for you. It's for the best."

I couldn't speak. I looked at Mama for a harsh word towards him, a glare, anything that showed that she didn't agree with a word of what he had just said. She had called me the kingdom's new hope, she said she wanted me back.

"Mama?" I choked meeting her eyes. Her hands tightened around mine, her eyes holding so many apologies, so many regrets. Was I one of them? There would be no problem if I hadn't been born.

"I'm sorry Teny," she whispered, wiping a tear that I didn't know had fallen down my cheek. It soon had a friend. "Truly, I am."

I didn't wait for another apology or justification. I got up without a bow, I pulled open the door, stepping out of the room trying to hide my sniffles. David was at my side in an instant. I didn't even glance at him. One look at my face and he would ask what was wrong and worst of all I would tell him. I said I wouldn't and I couldn't. For my family's safety. The family that lied to you and won't stop lying.

I shook my head. Don't think about that. Don't think about how my whole life had been a lie or how I would never be Queen of Xavia. That was what I was preparing for my whole life. Now I'd be remembered as the invalid princess who never became queen.

I didn't realise I had stopped in the middle of the corridor until David was standing in front of me shaking my shoulders. His lips were moving but I couldn't hear any words. I tilted my head to the side. Maybe I was sick. Maybe there was something really wrong with me. Maybe they were right, I wasn't ready and I would never be.

"Ria, please say something," David said, his voice muffled by some cloud of noise as he felt my forehead and the pulse in my neck and my wrists.

"David," I croaked coming out of my trance. I couldn't break. I couldn't tell him. "Yes, I'm here."

I breathed in. I wasn't heir anymore. I held the breath. I had been lied to. I exhaled. I'd protect what was left.

I drew a smile as I had always been taught to do.

"It's nothing really," I chirped, my cheeks pulling out unnaturally. "Just one of those days that I want to run away."

I gave a huge smile to reassure him. I honestly didn't believe that it did.

"All right Your Highness," he said warily, his hands slowly dropping from my shoulders.

I continued to smile even though I thought my face would crack. I walked along back to my room thinking about how badly I wanted to run away from the lies, from the masquerades, from the palace walls and from the air that was increasingly difficult to breath.

Chapter 25

My lessons continued as usual. I assumed they'd be less heavy now that I wasn't heir, but nobody knew that yet and they wouldn't for now. The words in my history textbook faded in and out of view even after my tutor left. I wondered if it was the effects of the alcohol. Or everything else. I slammed the book shut resisting the urge to throw it against the library walls. Did any of my ancestors go through half as much as I was? With wars and everything, they wouldn't have had time to be faking children's deaths and hiding affairs. Or maybe they did, but the book didn't think they were very important.

Why should who your father is even matter? Monarchy was the only job in the entire job in the world where it mattered. Where it could make or break you and right now, it was breaking me down to the core.

I got up gathering the rest of my papers and headed out the library doors. I was glad to be alone. For safety or not, having a person trail alongside me every minute of the day was entirely exhausting even more so now.

I looked at the ground and trudged my feet slowly, lost in my thoughts that I didn't even notice a familiar face walking towards me.

"James," I said as he attempted to stoop into a bow but I

stopped him. "Please don't."

"All right I won't," he said with a smile that slowly fell as he looked at me. "Is everything all right?" Was I frowning? What made him say that? I turned on the voltage on my smile.

"Of course, why wouldn't it be?"

He looked down at his feet a little sheepishly. "Alexander said you were in his room this afternoon."

I paused and hoped that was all he had said. I hadn't seen him after he had stormed out to face Mama and the prince. I didn't even know if he agreed with this whole new arrangement.

"I did," I replied stopping myself from tugging at the hem of my dress, "I wanted to bury the hatchet before he left." Before he inevitably moved in after the announcement.

James nodded but he didn't look too satisfied so I quickly changed the subject.

"How is Alexnder?"

James placed a hand in his pocket before replying, "I honestly haven't seen him since this morning."

So Mama and the prince were the last people to see him. I wondered why he wasn't with us when we were discussing the arrangement. Perhaps he was too upset.

"I didn't see him in the library either," I said thinking back to my hour and a half lesson. He could be anywhere really in this palace.

Before either of us could say another word a scream broke out from upstairs. We both turned to see Aisha stumbling down hair askew, her face ashy as she yelled to guards who had stopped mid-patrol.

"Get the queen now!" she screamed and at least four guards went upstairs to the queen's chambers while others tried to sooth the wailing assistant. I ran to her before she tumbled down the stairs. "Aisha what's wrong?" I asked trying to get her to face me, but she wouldn't, her eyes were fixed back upstairs from what she had ran from. I turned to James.

"Get her a drink of water!"

He didn't have to be asked twice. He dashed to the kitchen almost knocking over concerned members of staff.

More shouts echoed through the palace from upstairs. I immediately got up and followed them.

"Princess, no wait!" yelled Aisha, but I ignored her as I ran up to the past the royal living quarters to the floor above. The walls were a sombre yellow and the wooden floors had splinters. In other words, it didn't seem to be used very frequently.

Except today. Guards were stationed at the top of the stairs with others further down the hall. I saw David among them, but his eyes fell when he saw me.

He rushed over taking me by the hand preparing to lead me down.

"Aria, you shouldn't be here," he said, his eyes still going back to the end of the hall. On closer inspection, I saw my mother and the prince there. They were trembling in fear. Mama's face bloated with tears.

I pulled away from my guard and the others before reaching the window everyone had gathered around.

In that very second, I wished I had listened. I wished I had stayed behind downstairs, safe from the horror before my eyes.

Alexander. Cousin Alexander. My brother, Alexander. Unconscious. Hanging with a rope around his neck.

I backed away from the sight, as the doctors came along with the guards to bring his body down from the hook on the window.

Mama's sobs broke through the silent proceedings. The prince didn't cry. He just held my mother as his mouth hung open in abject horror and his eyes misted over as he kept saying, "My son, my son, why?"

I wanted to know that too. But, more importantly, I needed to know if...

"Excuse me," I said to a doctor. I couldn't recognise my voice anymore. "Will he be okay?" Please say yes. Say he wanted to end his life but failed.

The doctor shook his head, his eyes filled with pity. "I'm so sorry, Your Highness."

I couldn't move. I saw the deep gaudy scar on his neck when they were able to remove the ropes. If he had been found sooner. If I hadn't left him alone. If I had listened.

My body wracked with sobs as the doctor gestured to someone nearby.

"This is no place for her right now," he said, guiding me into the hands of my guard. "Please take her."

"Come on," David whispered, leading me back down the stairs. I hesitated for a few moments trying to regain my bearings. This was all just a bad dream. A trick. Alexander wanted to let off some steam and was playing a trick. The doctors could be in on it. They seemed to be good when it came to secrets.

We came to my room where I was met by Hanna, Petal and Miracle who got up from their work immediately. I could see from the expressions on their faces that it wasn't a dream. It was real. Alexander was dead. He had killed himself.

I nearly collapsed as I was moved to my chair so I leaned

forward to steady myself and to stop them from seeing my tears. This was all my fault. If I hadn't told him about my mother, then he might not have...

He knew so much already. Trusted too little. That as well as being declared heir must have been the final straw.

I choked and clasped a hand to my mouth. My poor cousin. He must have felt there was no escape from this.

"You're shivering," noticed Miracle going to get a wrapper to throw over me. It didn't change anything. I was still shaking, inside and out.

I muttered a thank you or what sounded like one. My sobs filled the room, bouncing off the walls and coming back to me in full measure. I hiccupped and almost fell out of my chair before Hanna steadied me.

I didn't know how long this went on for. An hour, or two or three before I was in my bed with too many blankets and Hanna, sitting on the chaise was watching me as she sewed.

Then she looked in her sewing basket and let out a sigh.

"Forgive me, princess," she said, attempting to get up. "But I'll have to get more thread. Will you be fine on your own?"

The pitying way she said this almost broke my heart. Did I really look that delicate?

"It's fine," I replied, shifting to look up at her properly. She was looking at me as if I would crack if I came out of this bed, "Go."

She lowered her head before coming towards my bed and began to stroke my hair. "It'll be alright, eh," she said. Why was everyone so intent on telling lies and half lies?

She gave me a reassuring smile before leaving the room.

I twisted in my bed. How were Mama and the prince feeling right now? They looked devastated but I couldn't help but blame them.

What in Ogun's name made them think it was okay to put that responsibility on Alexander. I could hardly handle it sometimes and I believed it was my birthright! And to find that the queen was actually his mother. I could imagine how he felt. Carrying all that weight on his shoulders. I held back another sob before turning to the door. There was something there brushed to the corner.

I got up, pushing away the covers and edged towards the door to see what it was. I bent down and saw it was a folded note with my name on it. I picked it up and sat on the edge of my bed. I took a deep breath as I unfolded it and began to read:

Cousin Imotenya,

I really don't know what to say but that you were right. Your mother is my mother too. Isn't that strange? I always suspected my father was having an affair with the queen. The amount of time she came to visit and the ridiculous number of events that we saw her at. I could never have suspected that you were a product of that. And then they wanted to continue to try so hard to hide their mistakes. Make me king. How funny. Since my father never got his dream, he tried to push it on to me. Well he won't be able to anymore.

I'm sorry if I offended you at all Teny, but that was planted in my head by my father. Our father. Sometimes I wonder if when people have kids, they have other human beings or do they just have mini-versions of themselves that they twist and pour on all their mistakes and failures. Do those mini-people ever break free? Maybe. But it wasn't happening for me.

Right now, I feel sorry for you Teny. You'll have to go through with the lie and the broken system. It doesn't even matter about the affair it's what they have been doing to keep it secret. Secrets are destroying this country. But if this goes according to plan, I know deep down you can handle it. You're braver than me cousin, not afraid to stand up for yourself. Don't ever lose that. Take care of our parents, you know they need it.

See you soon; hopefully, not too soon. Your cousin,
Alexander Best

My eyes were stung and I could barely see the words in front of me. I sunk deeper into my bed letting out a fresh stream of tears. Why did he write this to me? Why did he think it was important for me to know that and not our parents? He was wrong. I wasn't as strong as he thought I was.

I held the letter tightly in my fists as I rocked myself back and forth almost falling backwards. I thought of what my parents would say about this. They wouldn't want this to get out further than the four walls of this palace. If they had their way, no one would even suspect what had happened. Another lie, to add to our generous supply.

I fell back against the bed and stared at the ceiling's uneven marks. In all of this I had almost forgotten one implication: I was now the heir. For real this time. I bit my trembling lip. Someone needed to die to bring that about. I always thought it would be me and for a few harrowing seconds I was disappointed that I hadn't found a rope first. My brother would still be alive.

Chapter 26

I was left alone for a couple of hours more after Hanna came back. Mama and the prince didn't come to see me. They probably didn't know I knew about what happened. They barely noticed me at the window. They were too consumed by their own pain, their own grief and hopefully their own guilt. This was their fault. How could the prince not notice that there was something wrong with his son? That he was putting so much pressure on him. How could he betray his brother?

I threw a pillow at the window which moved the curtains allowing me to see the darkening sky. I supposed it was dinner time but I doubted that anyone would want to eat at a time like this. I certainly didn't feel like it.

Hanna got up without being asked and retrieved my pillow. She knew better than to scold me. She just placed it beside her on the chaise. I pressed my face against the pillow. I saw white specs that just annoyed me so I pulled my face out and faced the ceiling. Then the door. Then the window. Ceiling, door, window. Repeat.

There was a knock at the door. My eyes were still at the window. "I want to speak with her."

Hanna obeyed quickly and I saw that my visitor was the queen. I was tempted to go back to looking at the window but

I saw that Hanna had left me alone with my mother. I sat up, wiping my eyes. I would hate to see what I looked like and I had never considered myself a particularly vain person.

Mama didn't look any better. She looked as if she had cried from noon until now and her hands were shaking as if she could feel the blood on them.

"Imotenya," she said her voice wobbling and her knees about to give way before she sat down beside me.

"Oh, my dear!" she sighed, taking me in her arms. I began to cry again. She had not lost only a husband but a son as well. All through her mistakes. I think that made it all worse. It could have been avoided. Her tears trickled down my neck as I felt her tighten her grip on me.

I didn't think about betrayals, the hurt I was feeling or anyone who was against our reign. I just sat there. Probably the last bit of sitting I would do for a long time.

After Mama left, I remained once again, curled in my bed. She didn't say anything before she left and neither did I. What could we say? It was worse than finding out that my father-or who I thought was my father, since there was no happy reunion to tamper the sadness of his passing.

It was late evening by now and the sky looked darker than usual from my open window. It was as if the moon knew not to shine tonight and in return, I wouldn't sleep tonight.

I got up and noticed that I was still in my day clothes but I wasn't in the mood to change. I paced around being careful not to look at my desk. I had left Alexander's note there and was still debating whether I should tear it up or not. There was no chance that I would show my parents. If Alexander wanted them to know how he felt then… I didn't know what he'd do.

I turned to the door, feeling suffocated by my thoughts. I needed to get out of here. I pulled the door open and addressed the two guards that were standing there.

"I will be going for a walk," I said flatly. "and I will not need an escort." I turned down the hall before either of them could answer. I strode down the hall past Mama's room. I wondered if once again she had cried herself to sleep or had foregone sleeping all together, in favour of regret.

I quickly went down to the next floor, starting to regret not putting on slippers. I glanced down the hall to the guest bedrooms. My uncle was in one of those rooms mourning his son while his son's room was now empty. I felt sorry, despite everything he did truly want what was best for his son. No matter how far he was willing to go to get it.

I held back a tear as I continued downstairs. The tiled floors of the ground floor were freezing, so I hopped from foot to foot as I headed down the hall, staring at portraits of ancestors past.

Someday, God willing, I'd be up there too. There was almost no doubt about that now.

"Princess?" a voice whispered from behind me. It was James coming up from the kitchens.

I could see that he was contemplating a bow as he shifted the cup he was holding to his other hand.

"Is that for my uncle?" I asked, gesturing to the cup.

"No," he replied quickly looking nervous, "I needed a drink because…" He didn't finish his sentence. I wouldn't even have allowed him.

"I'm so sorry, Aria. I didn't notice anything was wrong with him. I swear, I…"

His voice broke then he took a deep breath. "I didn't know him very well and not very long but he seemed nice enough. He looked lonely though, I didn't think that he could..."

I gulped. "It's always the people that look fine, you'd suspect if they weren't." He looked at his feet then at me. Then he handed me the cup.

"Here, you need it more than I do."

I shook my head wrapping my arms around myself. "No, it's yours."

"Come on," he urged, pushing the cup in front of me. I took the cup from his hands and took his sip. It was hot chocolate with a hint of something bitter. I hoped against hope that it wasn't alcohol, it would drive me to a dark place.

"Thank you," I said quickly before I'd start crying again.

"It was my mother's recipe. She used to make it all the time when my brother died." His golden eyes glossed over as he scratched the back of his neck. "I know the circumstances are different but I kind of felt the same."

"Then you need this," I said, almost giving the cup back to him but he gave a grim smile. "I'm fine that was supposed to be my second cup."

I never thought of how what happened would affect James. He knew him too, longer than I did. "So what are your plans for after you go back to Lagos?"

He shoved his hands in the pockets of pyjama bottoms and lowered his eyes as if he hadn't thought about this before.

"My term was for the summer until... until Alexander went back to school."

"Oh." I began to feel awful for asking.

"I suppose his Highness may keep me on to do some odd tasks for him but... it will feel different." I nodded. It had only been a couple of hours but I could feel the loss as if he had been gone for fifty years. I focused on the chocolate powder granules that were swirling around at the bottom of the cup.

"I can't believe he's gone." My throat closed painfully and the granules began to look like they were in an ocean. "We didn't get along but he didn't have to go, not like that."

All that could be heard in the hall was my sniffles. James stepped cautiously towards me and placed an arm around my shoulder. I leaned into the crook of his neck.

"Hey," he whispered. "You guys were family and family fights. I bet he knew that you did really care about him, in your own way."

Did he? If he believed I or any of his family cared, then why did he do it? Did he not believe our parents could be reasoned with? But I knew better. They were both stubborn people and if something stood in the way of their plans, they removed it as they would Mariad Okode anytime soon.

I cried harder then, borrowing my head in the crook of James's neck as he hushed me. That was probably another thing Alexander knew. Everything our parents did to keep the throne. I understood that I didn't know half of it.

"How did it get to this?" I murmured, hugging the still warm cup to my chest. I really wanted to know if there was a moment in either my life or anyone else's that would have stopped all of this from happening. I could think about myself not being born into this family or even perhaps that my ancestors didn't overthrow the Korades before them. Who knew what all our lives would be like without the chains of ruling a nation? Who would want the burden of that?

"Aria? What are you doing here?"

I turned to the voice behind me and saw David standing right there in a shirt and khaki trousers with a holster at his belt. His face was etched with worry, from what I could make out through my teary eyes.

"She couldn't sleep," James answered, removing his arm from my shoulder and helped me stand up. I turned to my guard who was looking at me for confirmation. I gave a weak nod. I didn't want to start crying again so I gave James back his cup and touched his arm in thanks. He gave me a serene smile in return before David guided me up the stairs to my room.

The guards weren't there which meant they had gone to look for me. Probably to make sure that I didn't repeat my cousin's actions. David had been looking at me from the moment he had found me to the moment we came up.

"Aria, if you need to talk about anything," he said his eyes downcast. "I'm right here."

I rubbed my eyes. "I think we're past talking." I wanted to talk. To him to anyone but mostly to him.

Without warning, he took me in his arms hugging me close. His chin rested on the top of my head as he muttered, "I'm so sorry, my little dove. That you had to see that."

My heart clenched in my chest. If he knew all the things that I'd seen and that I know, he would weep a river for me. I felt so weak, so broken. At that moment David was the only thing that was keeping me afloat. When we pulled apart my head was swimming. I couldn't think straight so I pulled him back and placed his lips on mine. As I always imagined they were soft but firm and by some extraordinary miracle, they were kissing mine back. My arms wrapped around his neck pulling him closer, deeper while his hands trailed against the thin fabric of my dress. He pushed me against the wall hitching my dress up. I moaned against his lips edging him on, but then he stopped and promptly let go of me. I nearly fell on the floor without his arms holding me as his hand went to his lips in shock and disgust about what had just happened.

"I'm sorry," he said, backing away from me, horrified. "I didn't mean to… you don't need that right now and it can't happen again, I'm sorry."

I edged towards him. He couldn't be saying that. If anything, it was my fault. All of it was my fault. Everything that had happened.

From behind his shoulder, I could see my guards coming back from their search. Without another word or terrible mistake I slipped into my room and shut the door. I stumbled to my bed and cried quietly into the pillow. Stupid, stupid, stupid. What was I thinking? But he had kissed me back, didn't he? I wasn't imagining that.

I furiously shook my head and cried harder. I was a horrible human being. My brother had just died in one of the most horrible ways possible and here I was thinking about whether or not my guard had enjoyed kissing me or not. I pulled the pillow over my face hoping that for a few more hours I would not make another fatal mistake.

Chapter 27

When I woke there was a solemn atmosphere around the palace. It was as if we had gone back to the day of the king's death. I was put in another black dress with a veil. I had a feeling I would need it today.

"There," Miracle said as she helped me into my shoes. I was embarrassed that I needed her for such a simple task but I couldn't help it. I felt so weak, so stiff that I wasn't sure if my body was under my control.

"Thank you," I said as she gave me a weak smile and went back to place my night-clothes in my wardrobe.

There was a knock and I moved to answer it, expecting it to be David coming to escort me to breakfast. Instead I saw Avery standing there.

"Sorry princess but Officer Soro has taken ill and I will be taking his duties for today," he said with an apologetic look on his face.

"Oh," I said looking down at my feet. David, in all the years I had known him, had never gotten sick. He obviously didn't want to see me after what had happened last night. I held back tears. I was driving him away. What had I been thinking?

"Princess, are you ready to go down?" Avery asked, looking worried.

"Ah, yes."

I walked past him, lengthening my strides as best I could so I could get down quicker. When I got there the dining room was empty. Uncle may be preparing to leave and Mama, well. Mama was probably helping him or still in her room. I didn't want to stay in there longer than I had to. I didn't even have an appetite.

I rushed back out almost knocking over Avery. I went back down the hall to see servants moving boxes outside. In the midst of them stood the prince as I had never seen him before.

His cocksure look was gone, replaced with utter despair that pressed upon his shoulders. He leaned heavily on his cane as he absentmindedly gave orders to the servants. One of them was James. Our eyes met and he gave me a smile. I didn't say a proper goodbye to him yesterday so I mouthed a sorry, but he just shook his head easily. I would miss him. I turned to the prince who was staring into space.

I had to speak with him. I ran over then bent into a curtsey.

"Uncle," I said, drawing out the word for emphasis. "I'm so sorry about Alexander." He just nodded and went back to overseeing his luggage. Then he turned to me with bloodshot eyes and a face that looked years ahead of its age.

"Come with me," he rasped. He began walking towards the living room as Avery came and stood at his side. He was less subtle and tactful than David. I grimaced. I shouldn't think about him now.

"Stand outside. I'll be out in a minute." He looked a little astonished as if he was going to argue with me, but I had followed my uncle inside. He fell ungracefully into a chair and drew a hand across his face. I sat down opposite trying to and failing to stop my hands from pulling at my dress. Maybe I should ask if I could start wearing trousers.

"Imotenya," the prince began but he seemed more preoccupied with the painting of my grandfather behind me. Perhaps he was wondering if he would be proud of him.

"With this unfortunate turn of events," he said, his voice shaking, "Things are as they had been in the beginning."

I nodded. Then I thought it over in my mind. It wasn't like that necessarily. There were still some that supported his ascent then with the law change, Patience would be his heir. I could have laughed at the irony. The law change that was supposed to lead to my ascent, could end up not even helping me to the throne. I then thought of all those who knew the truth. Maybe it had slipped out and the chiefs who knew were the ones who supported the rebels had started the campaign to not let an illegitimate child on the throne.

"Things can never be as they were in the beginning Uncle," I replied, crossing my arms.

"I know."

"Well, it's settled then. I'm the heir." The words were meant to bite but it sounded like a whisper. The prince's eyes met mine sharply. His breaths were deep and quick.

"Nothing is settled my dear. It never was."

"How? The only other option was Alexander."

The man in front of me was clever and manipulative. So many people couldn't have come to his side without that. We thought our enemy was the people outside but we were wrong. The enemy was in our family. I had to hope against hope that I could throw him off. Even in grief, he never ceases to scheme.

"But he didn't want it," I continued starting to tear up. "He didn't want to be king, did he? But you didn't care. If this rebellion for some reason failed, you wanted to get your son on the throne by legitimate means."

He was starting to shake, his hand gripping his cane as if it was a life-line.

"But he knew that there was so much about you. How you cheated on who he thought was his mother. Poor Auntie Patience. She had to pretend that someone else's child was hers, while her husband had a child with another woman."

He snapped and stood placing a hand on my neck. I gasped as his eyes blazed and he said, "That's enough Imotenya."

"That's why he did it. He was tired of the lies, the oppression that you and Mama put on him." His grip tightened. My hands were on his trying to push his hand off but it was no use.

"Don't you ever talk about my son again!"

He pushed me back against the sofa, finally letting me go. I touched my throat, happy to get my taste of air.

He paced back and forth muttering to himself. "Alexander was weak."

No, he wasn't. He was stronger than the prince would ever be. Before either of us could make another move the door opened and in stepped Mama in a white dressing gown. Her eyes were still swollen and her hair was a mess.

"What's going in here?" she asked her voice at the point of breaking.

"Nothing Mama," I replied. "I was just saying goodbye to Uncle."

I gave a bitter smile as I stepped out of the room but the smile faded when I walked past the front door. I saw a stretcher. I didn't need anyone to tell me who was on it. He was placed in the back of a vehicle to be taken to the airport where he'd be flown back to Lagos.

I gulped and lowered my head in respect. It was all I could do for him now.

Mama and the prince came out soon after in a deep conversation. When Mama caught my eye she immediately turned away and went back to talking. They walked past me into the compound to the car. I didn't dare follow. I saw Mama place her hand on the prince's shoulder and whispered supportively and when she had finished, he looked around then kissed her hand.

I stood there gaping. Lucky Accra wasn't just her brother-in-law that she had a child for. He was the man she loved. Not the King. I wondered why she married him then but then I realised that it was an arrangement. That was the thing about this life. It can hand everything to you. Everything except love and sometimes you looked for it elsewhere. No matter how wrong that elsewhere may be. That elsewhere was tearing us apart.

"Goodbye Lucky," I heard Mama say as the prince stepped into the car and with one last wave goodbye, it drove towards the main gate.

He was gone. I used to think that when he left, I would be losing a pernicious uncle who was vying for his chance at the throne. Instead, I lost my father. Or did I just lose a man who impregnated my mother and didn't care a thing about me? It hurt less to think of it that way. After a few minutes Mama walked back inside with her head down.

"We have a meeting with the chiefs today," she said flatly as servants bowed on her way up the stairs. I sprinted to keep up with her.

"Today?" I asked. "Are you sure that's a good idea Ma?"

She didn't turn back but just kept going until she reached our corridor. She went into her room.

"Don't be late," she replied coldly before slamming the door in my face. I was left alone standing in the corridor pathetically in front of my mother's door. I wanted to cry. The prince told her what I said and now she was angry with me. What had I been thinking? What good could have come out of confronting him like that?

I clasped a hand over my mouth as a sob escaped. I couldn't believe what had happened in the last few days and all I wanted to do was talk about all of it with my best friend. Who wasn't even attending to me, and who I was sure wanted nothing to do with me. I closed my eyes and leaned back against the wall. Just to think that a week ago, I was in Sapele with my foster family. Far away from my duties as a princess. I knew that it would come for me one day, but it wasn't something I thought about. If I knew how things would get, I would have never complained, when village boys kicked sand up at me, or when Winter wanted to look at the presents I received from the palace or when Ma Osa told me to sweep the floor in the morning. Right now, those were the moments I treasured most.

"Princess?"

My eyes shot open at the voice. Petal was standing there, her eyes wide with worry. I quickly wiped my face and smiled but it didn't fool her.

"Your Highness, is everything all right?" she asked, taking my hand and guiding me away from the wall. I wanted to push her hand away but I didn't. I had already pushed two people that I cared about away, I was not going to risk a third. So I shook my head and leaned into her embrace.

I sighed. "It's just that something like that should happen here. It's awful. I don't even know why he would do it."

I knew very well but Petal didn't need to know why.

Petal didn't say anything. She let me rely on her tall and willowy frame all the way back to my room before she said, "I don't know what Sir Alexander was going through but I'm sure now he's at peace. That's all you can do princess."

I nodded. She was so sweet. I gave a weak smile before we went into my room. I went towards my desk to get a notepad for the meeting while Petal took up a piece of sewing on the chaise.

"What are you making?" I asked about craning my neck but Petal nervously turned away.

"Hanna said it was supposed to be a surprise," she said quietly and I nodded. "And we wouldn't want to upset Hanna, would we?"

She chuckled softly before threading her needle. I felt a little better and I almost forgot I had a meeting in an hour. Almost.

I went to the administrative building about fifteen minutes earlier than Mama so I could appease her. I wandered around touching the carvings and creating my own shapes.

"Beautiful, aren't they?

I quickly turned around to see an old man smiling down at me. It was Chief Oluwade. "Good morning Your Highness," he said standing straighter with his cane.

"Good morning Sir," I replied wondering why he was here alone. "If I may ask why are you alone, aren't the others coming today?"

"Oh today," he said scratching his chin. "Today is not a general meeting. A few of us have some things that we need to discuss with the queen."

I nodded and looked at the door of the meeting room. It hadn't changed since last week but maybe I'd have a chance to go inside this time. I would have to eventually.

"I heard the news," Chief Oluwade said his voice now sombre. "Condolences."

I nodded. "Thank you."

"Oluwade."

We both turned to see my mother coming into the building with two men beside her. Chief Agoto and Chief Benson I believed. They both greeted me in turn and gave me the necessary condolences. I hadn't heard so many in my life as I heard in this past week.

"Shall we go in?" Agoto offered, already moving towards the doors where the guards stood. "Of course," replied Mama following him along with Oluwade and Benson behind her. I waited for my invitation to follow.

Mama looked back and said, "Imotenya, come." She didn't look back to see if I would. I walked over, trying to keep my head held high as I could without it starting to feel like a burden especially with the way Mama was treating me. I couldn't think about that now, I had to face these chiefs.

There was a long table with red cloth in the middle of it. There were jugs of water along the length of the table as well as orange tumblers. There were even bowls of fruit, although I couldn't understand how somebody could eat at a time like this.

We all sat down, with Mama at the head of the table. I sat at her right hand and the Chief's all sat to her left. It felt like any major decision happening here today should in theory be discussed by more people but I felt no matter how important today's discussion would be, it had to be confidential.

"Will the princess stay for the meeting?" asked Chief Agoto observing me, daring me to make a wrong move. I met his eyes with an iron gaze. All my manners lessons had not been for naught.

"I don't see why not," Mama quipped, once again not looking in my direction. I didn't know how long I could take much more of this.

"Well, let us begin," Mama finally announced with the clap of her hands, after which, she flipped through some papers she had brought with her. I instantly regretted not taking a biro and note book. I didn't wish to see how unprepared I looked so I just folded my hands neatly on my lap. "My queen," Chief Benson began. "We wanted to once again give our condolences on the eve of this tragedy. Especially as it occurred when our king hasn't yet been buried in the ground."

He spoke as if two people dying within a week of each other wasn't a strange thing. I wondered if they knew Alexander's death had been suicide. I didn't think to ask what we would tell everyone. With our history, I didn't think the truth would cut it.

"Thank you," Mama replied quickly as if impatient to get on with today's business. "Now, what is it that we are actually here to discuss?"

All the chiefs looked at each other in turn before Agoto spoke up.

"Your Majesty, I want to say that Mariad Okode was meant to be here today but a sudden burst of illness prevented him."

Mama pursed her lips. I wondered if she knew about this "sudden burst of illness".

"The poor man," she said, tapping her lip with her biro. "I pray he gets better soon." I couldn't help but hear, "I hope he gets put out of his misery soon."

"Yes." Agoto scratched his nose and eyed the jug of water. "But that is beside the point."

"The point being," Benson interrupted. I tightened the grip on my hands, "That he had made some shocking revelations."

Mama and I took all the air out of the room. The bastard. He hadn't given his word but he had kept it for all these years but now he had chosen to reveal it. I'm not sure the way he was kicked out of the palace helped in any way.

"What revelations?" edged Mama cautiously. I could tell she was ready to shut down any argument.

"That payments have been made to rebel states in the last six years out of the royal treasury." My shoulders relaxed. He didn't tell them that. But now we had another problem to deal with. The money out of the royal treasury.

"Preposterous," scoffed Mama leaning forward in her chair. "What made him say such a thing?"

"It was implied by the Head of the Treasury," continued Agoto. "That a considerable amount of funds has gone to various different personal accounts recently."

"Money was sent to the Srahans in Sapele to care for my daughter, yes. I can't see why that is a problem." She was glaring at them each, daring them to make another accusation. It was if she had grown used to them.

"That isn't a problem," said Benson, folding a sheet of paper. "And I believe they will continue to be compensated for their efforts but those were already looked into. The money was going to unnamed personal accounts that were suspected of being the rebel chiefs."

"I see," Mama said arching her fingers in thought. Then she stared at them with a gaze of steel. "And why would I be supporting people who want my family dead? Who caused me to lose years with my daughter?"

"Forgive me, Your Majesty," Agoto interrupted. "But it wasn't just the rebels that you wanted to protect the princess from. There was also the case against the prince, whom you have kept under your roof this past week."

Mama was seething. "Are you saying that for whatever reason you've concocted, you don't trust my judgement or my loyalties? It is true that some of the former members of our council didn't approve of the law change that would allow Imotenya be heir. They'd rather it went to the prince. But I assure you he has made his intentions quite clear. He didn't show any support for the defectors that claimed to be on his side. And need I remind you Sirs, that some of those rebels are not interested in backing their favourite royal. Oh no, they want to take this country to hell in a basket and it is divisions like this. All these rumours, suspicions and general instability are what are making these people get a foot hole in this country."

I would have applauded her if I didn't know half the things I did. But she was right even if she was being a hypocrite about it.

"I see your point," Oluwade said then turned to look at me with a broad smile. "At least we can say that the princess's address had an effect on the people."

I tilted my head. "What do you mean, Sir?"

"I mean to say you have inspired people to action. There are reports of people setting up their own watches in the towns."

I held back a grin at that. I was glad to know I had actually done something good while I was here. It hadn't been a complete tragedy.

"Well, as we were saying," Agoto huffed. "We just wanted to be sure where all the kingdom's finances are going."

"Not to fund rebel causes I assure you," said Mama plainly. "For all we know, the Head of the Treasury could have put the recordings in the family account by mistake. I wouldn't put it past him."

All three of the chiefs nodded in agreement, but Agoto didn't look too satisfied.

"And besides," Mama added. "I don't understand what business any of the Chiefs have with the Head of the Treasury. I believe queries have to be passed through the monarch or who is standing in his place."

Agoto and Benson looked sheepish, but Oluwade stood his ground.

"My queen, it is often that there is such a long gap between the death of one monarch and the succession of the heir."

I gripped the edge of the table and prayed that they were

not in fact talking about the succession at a time like this.

"Well it is not often that a female child is pronounced heir," Mama replied folding her arms, "And yet here we are."

Oluwade nodded, pinching at his beard and taking down a note.

"After the funeral, we will look towards the coronation of our future queen." Future queen. It couldn't be more real if it was written in stone.

None of the chief's faces betrayed any doubt or concern. It was just blank acceptance and it made sense since they weren't holding guns at our heads.

"Then it is settled then," said Benson with his hands on the table before declaring, "Ohe'Imotenya."

"Ohe'Imotenya," Agoto and Oluwade responded. It was real. I would finally be queen.

I gave a neutral look, neither glad nor sad, as befitting the circumstances.

"I will strive to live up to my father's legacy," I said resolutely and I would. I may not have been supposed to be here but I was and now I'd have to make do.

And without another word, I looked at Mama and she almost looked pleased with me. Almost. After about half an hour sorting out logistics before the meeting was officially closed. We all rose after the queen and said our goodbyes.

Before I could follow my mother out, Chief Oluwade called out to me. "Your Highness, may I speak with you for a moment?"

I looked around to see my mother and the other chiefs had already left the hall, leaving me alone with Oluwade and the guards at the meeting room door.

"Of course, Sir."

"I'll be brief. I just want to once again apologize for what happened to your cousin. I can't imagine what you're going through."

I nodded, not really wanting to talk about this again. I really didn't want to cry again today. "My daughter is a huge fan of yours and was shocked when she heard the news."

"Your daughter?"

"Yes, my youngest. She was devastated when she heard the news of your cousin and asked me to give you this."

He reached into his pocket and pulled out an embroidered handkerchief. It was a thick white thing with my family's crest of a golden eagle rising in the sun on the right and my initials I.A in red thread on the left.

"She made this herself?" I asked in awe. Embroidery had never my strong suit, that had more Judith's expertise.

"Yes, she's quite the tailor now," he said looking impressed. I smiled. I could tell by the way he talked about her that he loved her very much, "And she wanted to give you something as a welcome home present as well."

"Tell her thank you for me," I said, admiring the handiwork.

"I will, but I'm sure the best thanks she could receive would be an invitation to your birthday." I gulped. "Honestly, with everything that's happened I don't know if I feel like celebrating."

"I understand."

He reached for my hand and gave it a light shake.

"I pray for strength for you for this time, I believe you will need it, Your Highness," he said earnestly.

How right he was.

Chapter 28

The doors to my room were a welcome sight even though I had seen them this morning. Mama hadn't said anything about me working with her today, she just gave me a stack of papers but didn't say anything about what I was supposed to do with them or when we would discuss them.

I was positive she just wanted to feel like she was preparing me while dealing with her own grief.

She went straight to her room before I could see the tears threatening to fall down her face as she dabbed at her eyes with a black handkerchief. She had been wearing black for so long. We both had.

I flung the papers on my desk and sat on my bed. I was glad to be alone. After yesterday, it was a miracle that I got through that meeting. Or it would be if I still believed in miracles. I shut my eyes tight. I would not cry.

I opened them quickly and leaned back against the headboard. I needed to get out of my room or else I would spend the whole afternoon crying. I got up and went to my wardrobe. I could have rung for Petal or Miracle, but I wanted the satisfaction of putting on shorts and a shirt by myself. I found the flattest pair of shoes I could find and went downstairs to the gardens for a run.

I hadn't had a proper one since I had arrived at the palace. I couldn't think of a better time than now. I got down on one knee after a few stretches done under the watchful eyes of the guards. I counted myself in and then shot off.

Running had always been a release for me when I was studying or having tutors over. It made me feel free as if in control of life. It felt different here. Though I couldn't see them immediately I knew there were walls surrounding the palace compound not like Sapele's open air, with the white sand underneath my feet. It felt so artificial here but it would have to do.

I pumped my arms and took deeper breaths in through the mouth. David used to hammer onto me about the importance of pacing myself but I always ignored him. I didn't run to endure, I ran to fight off things, such as thoughts of my guard. I lengthened my strides as best as I could while my lungs burned. Flowers and bushes whizzed by. Their colours and scents blurred seamlessly into one another as I was in a new world where nothing of concern existed. But I began to slip out on my second lap as my legs gave way and lungs felt as if they absorbed blood.

I fell in red sand back first. I sneezed as some got into my nostrils but I didn't care. The physical discomfort was better than any emotional ones I would feel. I was ready to go again, when a maid came running out towards me.

I didn't get up, she could have been giving a message at the other end of the palace for all I knew but she stopped near and bowed as she was catching her breath.

"Princess," she heaved, placing a hand on her stomach. I sat up shielding my eyes from the harsh midday sun, "You're needed in the throne room immediately."

I tilted my head. The throne room was only used for special occasions or when special judgements were to be passed.

"What for?" I asked, moving my legs to a more comfortable position. They were starting to feel numb.

"I don't know Your Highness, only that the Queen asked for your presence as soon as possible." She seemed anxious as if she thought I would not agree to come with her. I honestly didn't want to, but I couldn't disobey the queen's orders.

I reached out my hand towards the girl and she pulled me up effortlessly. I told her I would follow after I had changed. In mourning or not, one did not go into the company of a queen in clothes covered in sweat and sand.

When I had changed back into my mourning dress, Miracle and Hanna were the only ones in my room. They got me changed quickly but didn't answer any of my questions. Hanna as always, continued with the task at hand. Miracle looked continually bothered, dropping things and muttering under her breath. None of them said anything about Petal.

The throne room was the biggest room I had seen so far in the palace. It had two thrones at the end of the room and tables with advisors seated at them along the sides. It was a deep shade of red with two gold and silver chandeliers hanging from the ceiling. It was worthy of the title of throne room. Guards stood along the walls at attention as I walked, self-conscious of the baby hairs coming out of my bead crown, to the top of the hall where Mama sat conversing with one of her advisors. Aisha stood in the corner failing to stop biting her nails. I smiled at her but she just turned away. I sat down on the small throne beside Mama as the advisor left her side.

"What's going on Mama?" I whispered taking into account the worried whispers and the tense glances around the room.

Once again, she didn't look at me.

"You'll see," she replied standing up and I followed her straightening my dress.

"Ohe'Igohmena, Ohe'Imotenya!" a herald cried out. "Ohe' Ighomena, Ohe'Imotenya," the room exploded.

I gave a weak smile as we sat back down and one of the advisors stepped from behind his place at the table and knelt at the throne.

"Rise up," Mama said and after a few minutes he did. Mama leaned forward in the throne and gestured for him to talk.

He cleared his throat and began to speak.

"Your Majesty, I wish to inform you that the documents from the King's office have been found." It was all I could do not to jump out of my throne. I hadn't heard anything about any missing documents. I hadn't even seen any documents in the room. All the cabinets were empty. Then I remembered that there was a drawer in the desk that I hadn't checked because it was locked. "Oh really," Mama said.

"Yes," he replied and he gestured to a servant who handed him a red file with the words confidential written across. Without warning, Mama rushed over to take it from his hand. She anxiously flipped through them, seeming satisfied, and thanked him and went back to the throne. "Where was it?"

The advisor straightened his back.

"It was found in the rooms of one of the servants."

Then he turned to a door with guards stationed at the side

of the room. As if on cue, they opened the door.

I gasped and got off the throne even as my mother tried to pull me down.

Two guards were dragging someone who had been beaten into the throne room. They could barely lift up their head but from the side, from their glossy hair and willowy frame I knew. It was Petal.

I clasped a hand over my mouth as Mama forced me back into my seat. I almost didn't notice that David had walked into the room behind the horrific sight. Our eyes met for a second as I tried to understand what was happening but he turned away as soon as he could. I grabbed on the arm of the throne to steady myself as the advisor went on speaking.

"Working on knowledge given by Officer Soro, there was a search of all the rooms in the servant's quarters. The diary was found in this girl's possessions."

Petal's head was jerked up by the guards and it took all my self-control not to yell in her defence. Someone could have planted the diary there for Ogun's sake! Although I don't know who or why they would do such a thing.

"This girl was in charge of my jewellery," Mama said looking closer at Petal as if she didn't recognise her. "She must have taken the key from the drawer."

I thought back to what I had seen of Mama's jewellery and there was one necklace that she wore often that had a straight bead on it. Then I remembered the lock of the drawer in the office. It was straight too.

But that didn't mean anything. There was no clear line directing to Petal. Not sweet, gentle, loyal Petal.

"Do you plead guilty?" asked Mama sharply. This was nonsense, of course she was innocent. I wanted nothing more than to jump to her defence but then two words came from down below that shook me to the core.

"Pleading guilty." Petal raised her head as far as she could with the guards holding her down. I saw something in her eyes that I had never noticed before. A strong resolve, a fire, an anger. Murmurs rose from the crowd of advisors.

The head advisor raised a hand to silence them.

"And was it you Petal Baucha that went into the princess's room and destroyed it?" he asked. Destroyed was a strong word to use. I was wondering how on earth I was still sitting upright, even more so when I heard Petal's reply.

"I was." There was no shame, no remorse. It was plain as day. She was owning up to thrashing my room.

That meant it was her who wrote the note. My stomach clenched. I didn't want to believe it but why would she confess. Was she protecting someone? That sounded more like it.

"And how do you explain your actions?" the advisor playing judge said loudly. Petal bit down on her lip that was already starting to bleed.

"I'll explain my actions," she said, her voice uncharacteristically loud. I would have guessed it was from whatever the guards had done to her, but there was more. "When you and your government explain the oppression that you've put on the people all these years."

The room erupted into shouts as the guards and the head advisor rushed to get them into order.

"You use lies and your laws to cover up all your corruption."

Petal was mad. What on earth was she talking about?

"I am afraid you must be quite distressed," the head advisor cooed condescendingly. "You can't know what you're saying and it's clear you don't understand your actions."

He took two languorous steps towards her but she didn't even flinch.

"What would a serving girl have need of royal documents and why would she fit to destroy the princess's chambers."

That's what I wanted to know too. I wrung my sweaty palms as I leaned to hear what she had to say, all while praying that this was some bad dream I was having.

"I wanted to make a statement and let everyone know the secrets that this family is keeping." Shouts of treason rung out through the hall. I could tell one believed her. I didn't want to believe, but now that was not possible.

The head advisor called once again for silence. I had a feeling he would be doing that a lot if this went on any longer.

"And would you care to tell us, girl, what secrets?"

Petal's eyes immediately turned towards me. I felt naked and wanted nothing more than to sink into that imposing throne.

"You have laws, but those high up don't even obey them."

I tightened my hands as if my illegitimacy was written all over my forehead.

"Oga's of the court, the king before he died, he had his doubts as to whether the princess was actually his child."

My heart stopped but I wouldn't let it show. I turned to Mama, who I could see was unfazed by all of this as if she got those accusations every day. I looked back at David who was staring at me in disbelief.

"That is why she was sent away to keep anyone from knowing the truth. And he suspected that was why the queen wanted the law change. So, her bastard child would have the throne." Mama sat upright and yelled, "Enough!"

The guards holding Petal pressed her face down to the Lino floor, but she wouldn't go down easily.

"It's in the king's diary," Petal yelled back. "That and so many other things about this nation."

Her face hit the floor and I heard a faint crack. I had no sense to grimace. This couldn't be happening.

"That would be considered as treason," the head advisor announced, "Defamatory, libel." Treason. Defamatory. Those were the words Mariad Okode used in his letter to Mama. What would happen if the truth got out? However, now as I so helplessly realized the truth was out, thankfully, it seemed nobody believed it. Or at the very least they didn't show they believed it. "For that," the head advisor continued "The sentence is death."

I wanted to scream. The room resounded into murmurs of agreement. I doubt anyone who had any doubt about the monarchy felt comfortable right now. I knew I didn't.

There was a flicker of fear across Petal's face but it was quickly replaced by a certain resolve. As if she believed in what she did so much she was willing to die for it. But why would she die just because she said something defamatory about the royal family and that probably wasn't what she was looking for in the king's diary. He himself had no proof of the affair. There must have been something much more pressing that she had been looking for. Perhaps she had found it and was very good at being secretive.

"But," Mama said as the noise died down. Her expression was pained as she stood up off her throne clenching the diary close to her chest. "With the untimely and the unfortunate deaths of my husband the king and my nephew."

She gulped and then continued with a vengeance, "I do not want this time to be synonymous with death and destruction and with that your sentence will be ten years imprisonment."

I turned to see the scribe and the judge furiously taking down notes as Petal was dragged by her handlers out of the throne room. I slumped back in the throne as Mama sat back down. Petal, a traitor? I held back the tears in my eyes at the thought. Then anger hit me. How could she do such a thing after the palace had taken her in and had given her such an opportunity? I could have easily had her fired but I didn't. I clenched my fists, nails digging into my hands.

Mama rose up and walked out of the room with the gazes of the advisors and guards fixed on her. I followed her wary of the glances that I was receiving. Did they really believe what Petal had said? They didn't argue with the judgment or maybe they didn't want to do so in public. "Stop being so negative," I told myself as I followed Mama's flowing black dress up the stairs. Why would they believe a maid and any suspicions that the king had?

"Imotenya come in here," said Mama when we came to her room. After the day I'd had all I wanted to do was hide in my room, maybe cry until tomorrow but with the hard, queenly look Mama was giving I couldn't refuse.

I didn't want to remember the last time I was in her or even the last time I slept here. So much had happened since then. I took a seat on the couch in the living room while Mama went into her bedroom.

I took a glass of water as I heard Mama tell a maid to leave. Said maid came out and I saw it was Dessa who was clutching her broom and pan. That reminded me of another thing I didn't want to remember. Mama came back with a change of jewellery. She was wearing the necklace with the key charm. It was imperative that it didn't fall in the wrong hands again. Petal must have taken it when removing my things from Mama's room back to my own.

Mama held onto the key around her neck as she came and sat opposite me. I poured her a drink of water which she took eagerly. I scratched at my knees as the silence between us deepened. At last Mama broke it after she took a long drink of water.

"I don't know if I will regret not killing the girl," she said thoughtfully.

"Like you did with Mariad Okode?" I asked.

She narrowed her eyes at me and put down her glass. "He's not dead."

"Not yet at least."

She turned away. She didn't deny it. I couldn't imagine how it was done. Probably someone in the office who would have done anything the queen asked him. I'd have to admit it was very shrewd. Killing him slowly. If it was done right no one would suspect anything than that he had died of natural causes.

"What are you going to do with the birth certificates?" I asked. If the real ones still existed then people would continue to ask questions.

"I believe the one Mariad dropped was the only one. We have copies of the new one and everyone's general trust."

Her voice faltered at the last words, as if she knew if they weren't true anymore.

"I didn't think he suspected," she went on, her eyes looking distant. "I didn't think he would have cared."

I looked at her, shocked. "Why would you say that?"

"He suggested that his brother sleep with his wife. I wouldn't think he'd have thoughts on that area. But to think that it bothered him... Nothing distracted him from his duties."

There was a pause before I could understand.

"Not even you?" I said. That still didn't excuse what she did not in the slightest but perhaps I could understand her.

"This life Imotenya is not an easy one. Constant scrutiny, constantly being watched. Your life is never your own. It turns out it never has been."

I understood that. No matter what happened I would never be able to escape my family, my heritage. My birthright. Although now I wasn't so sure that it was mine.

If things planned out the way Mama and the prince had orchestrated nobody would ever suspect a thing. We could move on from this and move on with our lives as usual. The people would stop revolting sooner or later and everything would be just fine. I had to believe that. It was all I had now.

"I know it won't be easy but it has to be done," Mama said, taking her hands in mine. I looked and forced a bitter smile.

"Because it is our duty."

Mama tilted her head as if seeing me for the first time. I wouldn't be surprised if she was. We really didn't know each other and even though I had learned so much about her in these last couple of days I didn't know if I could love her as much as I could. Blood didn't make family, and understanding one another didn't make love. But I couldn't focus on what I didn't have, I had a job to do.

I put down my glass and headed straight for the door. Before I could touch the handle, Mama asked, "Are you all right; are you happy?"

I turned slowly and replied quietly, "I'd have to be." Then without another word I left the room.

Chapter 29

When I left to go to my room, I saw David standing by my door, furiously briefing the guards standing in front of it. I had never seen him like that. He always seemed like he was on the receiving end of orders and I had never seen him take a position of authority. It hurt seeing him like this. It hurt seeing him at all.

I was just about to turn away when I heard him call out. "Your Highness?"

He walked over to me quickly with a hard-to-read expression on his face.

"Officer," I choked out. I hated this formality between us. It was stifling and I wanted to get out of there immediately.

"Princess, the guards who were supposed to be on duty have been dealt with and a new rota has been set for your chambers which in future, will be strongly adhered to."

I could see in the setting of his jaw that he was trying to believe that himself.

"Thank you, officer," I replied with a forced smile before he could say another word but he gently touched my wrist and gave me an imploring look.

"We need to talk," he whispered.

I nodded. I saw the guards stationed at my door and came

up with an idea. I told them that David was going to make security checks around my room. They didn't have a chance to question or argue before we were inside my room.

I moved to the window and leaned against my desk. With the calming view of the palace from outside, nobody from looking at it would suspect anything that had happened the last few days. Not to talk of the last few years.

David moved closer, his eyes scanning everything in the room but me. I wrung my hands again eager to get this over with. I never could remember a time it was so hard for us to say a word to each other and even then, the silence was comfortable not suffocating.

"Aria," he began, not moving from his spot. "I'm sorry."

"About what? My cousin's suicide or the fact that my maid is being convicted of treason." He blinked and I shook my head. "I'm sorry. You have nothing to apologize for."

I looked down shamefully at my shoes. I noticed they were the ones I had brought with me from Sapele.

"I kissed you…"

"And I should have stopped you," David said quickly, running a hand through his hair. "I'm an adult and I should have shown some restraint. You were upset and didn't know what you were doing."

I still didn't look at him. I was terribly upset but I did know what I was doing. At the time I wasn't sure why. I'm not sure I knew why now. But he must have had reasons of his own for kissing me back. He wouldn't just take advantage of me in my despair. That must have been why he stopped. I wanted to slap myself. There I was, fantasizing again. I had to grow up. I had let go of this, whatever it was between us. It would never be. Not now that I was undisputedly heir to the throne.

So I nodded, agreeing with everything that he had said because it would hurt to think otherwise. He came closer and reached to put an arm on my shoulder. He smiled easily as he took my hand in his. It was large and callused but it felt perfect. He had to stop doing things like this. He said it himself, I didn't know if I could control myself especially now. So I moved back, modestly covering my bare shoulders with my hands. If I didn't know better, I would have seen a flash of hurt float through his eyes but it left just quickly as it had come.

"You might be a future queen, he said, folding his hands behind his back. "But you're still like a sister to me."

I smiled. "Your little dove?"

He smiled back. "I don't know if I can call you little anymore."

My mind jumped with conclusions and hidden meanings and all I wanted to do was shut it down. After a sideways hug he left my room and shut the door.

After a few seconds, I sank to the floor and clenched my eyes shut. I would not cry. I bit my lip as a tear came down my cheek for everything I had lost and all I had that I didn't want.

Chapter 30

Weeks went by in a string of lessons, reports and meetings. I tried not to think about anything that had happened the week I got back. Not death or stolen kisses. Fortunately, I didn't have to wear black anymore, but colour was so foreign to me that I couldn't help but request that all my outfits from then on be in shades of grey. Miracle saw to it immediately.

She had taken on the role of two maids now. I didn't want to ask for a new one if necessary but Miracle was extremely obliging. I liked her vivacity and enthusiasm which some days was all I had to get me through the day especially when Mama was late and showed up with puffy eyes and re-applied mascara.

"Amaka said that Chief of Bauchi's wife wore the same jewels the queen wore on her wedding day. It was so kind of the queen," She rambled as she braided my hair. I smiled and nodded wondering why a woman would give such a precious possession away. But then I thought that if what my mother told me was true, she probably didn't want another reminder of her unhappy marriage.

"It was really kind of her," I replied absent-mindedly as Miracle combed back my baby hairs. All the while, I couldn't stop thinking about Petal and what had happened to her. It seemed as if she knew the consequences for her actions, but didn't care because she had some sort of purpose in mind. One I couldn't understand.

"All done Princess," Miracle said, stepping back. Like always she had really outdone herself. The braids were done in a crown with golden beads along the locks. When the light hit off them it was as if light was radiating out of me, making me look much more regal than I felt.

I got up and straightened my dress before turning to Miracle.

"Thanks so much," I said, feeling delicately at her handiwork. She gave a smile that wasn't as bright as her usual ones. I could tell that recent events had had an impact on her too. She must be shocked about Petal but at the same time must miss her. I knew I did.

I left the room to begin another day at Mama's side. I'd have to admit that sometimes it was much better than the early morning mathematics lectures with Mr Zach. I was glad he was taking it easy on me because of everything.

When I came to the chamber which Mama had claimed as her temporary office, I saw that she wasn't the only one there. Chief Oluwade was there along with Chief Agoto while Mama sat at her desk. She waved me in and I bowed before turning to the chiefs who bowed in turn as I went to stand by Mama's side.

"Sorry I was late," I said looking at the chiefs. Oluwade had his ever-present smile while Agoto was in possession of his perpetual frown. I wondered if his face would split if he smiled.

"No bother, Chiefs Oluwade and Agoto were just leaving," she said flatly, as if the discussion hadn't been all that important.

Oluwade saw my confused look and said, "Just bringing reports from our states, Princess, nothing more."

I nodded, not entirely convinced.

"Well we must be going. Goodbye, Your Majesty."

With that, he and Agoto left the office space. They also left behind a very uneasy feeling in the atmosphere.

"What was that about?" I asked, going to get a stool from the corner of the room.

"They were talking about some intel about some dubious activity going on in their states." I put down the stool and sat crossed legged.

"Rebels?"

"Them but also some operatives from the north." I leaned forward.

"This isn't grounds for war is it?" I was worried. Now would be a good time to strike, especially if our leaders were going through a great personal crisis and the general instability.

"Not yet. Oluwade said they were surveying the land and he believes it was more than just checking the oil pipes."

"What are you going to do?"

Mama leaned back against the back of her chair.

"Well the advisors would say confront the King of Auja and tell him to get his operatives out of there," she mused.

"But what do you say we do?"

"I would say that we increase security along our northern border to see if they mean harm. Even if I were to speak with the king how do I know I'll receive a straight answer?"

"But with increased security along the border," I said. "Won't that leave the states with rebel activity without protection?"

I thought of the maps I had studied and remembered that most of the rebel activity was nowhere near the northern border. If our troops moved there, it would leave the southern states in the possession of the rebels.

"Things have quieted down there and besides it's not as if troops in the nearby states are static. They can easily be reassigned if need be."

Mama seemed to have her own plan in place but I couldn't help but feel uneasy. Or perhaps that was just me worrying for nothing or me hating the fact that my mother who was not of royal blood, made decisions for the nation now. I knew it was irrational but when you knew you were destined for something and that thing was no closer to coming true, well, the heart got sick and when it got sick it wanted awful things to happen.

I hummed in reluctant agreement as my eyes skimmed through the report on the desk. Out of the corner of my eye I saw a sheet with the title of burial arrangements.

The burial would be in a couple of days in the Valley of Kings in Ekewan road. It almost reminded me of Alexander's burial a few weeks back. It wasn't deserving of pomp and meticulous planning because of the circumstances. Almost a week after my father returned home my brother was buried. I couldn't help but feel that more than his body was buried that day. Truths and secrets were buried with the real heir of Xavia.

I blinked back tears. I had to stop thinking about that, I was the heir now. People died so this could come to pass. This crown was in front of me, I had to take it both hands or else someone would. And by God, they wouldn't let me live to see their succession.

"What do you need done Mama?" I asked mainly to distract myself from my thoughts but also because I genuinely wanted to do something.

Without missing a second, she handed me a pile of papers to stamp. I frowned. "Anything else for me to do?"

She shook her head while signing a document. "No."

I sighed and took out the stamps from the box. This would be a long afternoon.

After a lengthy stamping and signing session, I left Mama's new office and was on my way to the library. That had been my place of refuge for the past few weeks. Even in the short time I had been here, it held some happy memories. Especially of the first real friend I had made here.

I thought about James and how he was doing. I wished we had said a proper goodbye before he left. All I could remember was a fleeting look and me crying on his shoulder.

I hoped that he would come with my father to the burial. I could just write him a letter but with what happened with Alexander, I took a break from writing letters or even communicating with anyone outside the palace walls even my foster family.

I shook them out of my head as I walked through the silent halls. It was kind of refreshing not to have a guard trail behind me at all times especially not David. Even though I believed things were resolved between us I couldn't help but feel like there was a certain distance between us now. I couldn't remember the last time he had smiled at me or even discussed things that had nothing to do with our life at the palace. I missed that. I missed the us before all this.

When I came to the library, I saw that the door was already open, I peeked inside and saw Chief Oluwade standing next to a shelf of books inspecting the jackets while his mobile phone was at his ear.

"Okay, but what she is doing is completely irrational," he huffed to whoever was on the other end of the phone. "I should know, Jonathan."

After a few minutes of silence on his part before he finally said, "All right we'll be ready." He shoved the phone back into his pocket before skimming through the books again.

I slowly moved away from the door and backed towards the living chamber entrance.

It was obvious the "she" he was mentioning was the queen and the irrationality would have to be her decisions about the northern operatives. But who was Johnathan?

Suddenly, I saw Oluwade come out of the library and a guard approach him. I slipped into an alcove.

"Did you find what you were looking for Sir?" the guard asked. When he turned sideways, I saw it was Avery.

Oluwade smiled his signature smile. "Yes, I did," he replied. "I'm lucky that the King gave me permission to come to the royal library. My own is good but lacks when it comes to the classics."

"He must have been a dear friend," said Avery.

"Oh, he was. It's a shame how his life ended. At the height of his prime."

I should have been flattered to hear them talk about the way the man who I thought was my father, but something wasn't right.

I didn't like this at all, especially the way he was talking to Avery. It was as if they knew each other very well. But I couldn't see how.

I quietly edged deeper into the alcove as Oluwade and Avery walked past and shook hands.

I wanted to make a quick escape until I heard Avery say what Oluwade said on the phone to Jonathan. "We'll be ready, sir."

With that Oluwade nodded, and was shown out of the living quarters. I came out of the alcove in shock. Whatever it was they were discussing it had to be something important. Something to do with my mother. I backed away from the door and into someone. I quickly jumped around to apologize and saw that it was David.

He quickly bowed and said, "Sorry Princess," before going on his way. I immediately caught his wrist. I had to tell him what I had heard. I had made a mistake with Petal and look where that got us.

"David, I have to tell you something," I said, still holding his wrist. He frowned but didn't leave my grip. "What's the matter?"

I opened my mouth to speak but then found myself looking around to make sure that nobody would hear us. "Oluwade is planning something against the Queen," I said.

"What?" David replied in disbelief. "That's not possible. Why would he..."

"Because he disagrees with Mama about the way to deal with the northern operatives," I interrupted. He needed to understand how serious this was.

"Aria, he may disagree but that's no reason that he has to harm her."

"You don't know what I heard!" I nearly yelled then lowered my voice, leaning closer towards him. "He said to someone on the phone, Jonathan I think, that what the queen was doing was irrational and that they should be ready for something soon."

He gave a worried look but behind it I could see the scepticism behind his dark eyes. "You don't believe me," I huffed.

He sighed in annoyance, "No I do, it's just…"

"You told me I should have come to you when I saw the letter in my room. I'm coming to you now and you're just going to do nothing!"

David frowned and pulled his arm away. "I never said that."

"And another thing. He talked to Avery about this. Whatever he's doing Avery is in on it and who knows how many of the other guards."

A blind man could see the disbelief in his face.

"Avery? That can't be," he murmured. I didn't want to believe it myself. I had known Avery just as long as David, but with everything that had happened so far, I was beginning to lose trust in everyone I knew.

"I saw it with my own eyes David." In that moment more than ever I longed to tell him the truth. Why more than ever people around us would doubt our credibility. And it hurt that I couldn't. That I couldn't make him understand.

"It's all right. I'll see what I can do."

I sighed, taking a step back. "I'm worried David."

"Hey," he said, taking my hand in his. "Nothing is going to happen to you." I sucked on my lip and then gave him a small smile.

"Thank you."

He just nodded before bowing and going back to his business. I turned upstairs to go back to mine.

Chapter 31

Two days before the funeral we were to have a wake and almost all the family had arrived. Aunties Ayela and Oyela were at the palace along with Ayela's two daughters who were making disparaging comments about the lengths of the trousers of all the men in attendance. They had invited some of their friends as well for the food of course.

"Imotenya," called Auntie Ayela holding me tightly to her chest. "It's good to see you again."

"You too Auntie," I replied when she let me go. She was wearing a blue gele along with an aquamarine dress. She didn't have a glass of alcohol in her hand believe it or not but was rather taking long sips of water from a red tumbler.

"Well, how are you feeling?" she asked, adjusting her gele, "About your father and your cousin."

"I'm managing," I sighed. "Has the prince arrived yet?"

She looked taken aback at my question. In her mind, he was still the man that wanted the throne. Maybe he still was but that wasn't so clear anymore.

"I suspect he'll come later or better still on the morning of the burial."

I nodded and excused myself saying I needed to go see Mama about something. She just shrugged in reply and muttered something about getting something stronger. I walked along towards the entrance of the great hall. Extended family members I hadn't known about were there greeting me, offering condolences and asking to meet other family members, but I shut them all down. Most of them had only been here a couple of hours and yet they were already starting to get on my nerves. I eagerly looked around the room for any sign of the prince.

With a sigh, I turned back to the small party when the sound of an approaching car met my ears. I ran into the hall, but an onslaught of stewards from the living quarters beat me to it.

They stood attentively as the driver came out of the limo and opened the back door. Out stepped Prince Lucky wearing a pale red agbada with a black hat. He looked worse since the last time I saw him. Greys had multiplied through his hair and he leaned against his cane as if his life depended on it so much so that a steward had to hold onto him along with someone else who had come out from the car.

It was James. Once the prince was on his feet the steward let go, but James still held him. Suddenly, he pushed him off him with his cane and trapised all the way into the living quarters. I almost felt sorry for him.

James took two of his suitcases in his hands and made his way to the living quarters. Once inside I didn't know how long it would be until I had a chance to talk with him. So I ran towards him even at the risk of my gele coming loose.

He must have heard my footsteps because he turned around and smiled at me. It made me feel so much better.

"Hi," I said.

"Hello Your Highness," he replied with a solemn grin.

"I should leave you to it," I said. "Before my uncle realises, you're not there."

James suddenly looked like he remembered that he had a job to do. He hefted the bags and with one last smile, he tugged the suitcases up the stairs.

I smiled looking forward to when I could get a chance to speak with him again so much so I almost didn't want to leave. He really calmed me down last time.

With a sigh I turned around to go back into the administrative building when I heard my name being called. I turned and saw Mama and Uncle Lucky standing at the top of the staircase.

Mama was wearing a red dress similar to mine down to the skilfully wrapped gele instead of a crown.

As they came closer, I could see that Mama's lipstick seemed slightly smudged and her eyes looked as she had been crying. The prince looked just as he did a few moments ago but he straightened his neck and he had since discarded his hat. I gave Mama a curtsey and she nodded before turning to me and whispering, "You look beautiful."

"Thank you," I replied, still wary of the prince so nearby.

"How was your journey, Uncle?" I asked sweetly. He simply raised an eyebrow at my forced politeness.

"It was decent," he said, drawing a hand across his beard. I nodded as he offered Mama his arm and she took it when they started to walk out towards the administrative building. The evening air was cool on my bare shoulders and I thought I could smell a rain storm coming in. Koda taught me how to smell the air to track rain. Even if I couldn't do that, I knew it was almost the rainy season with the amount of water the palace kitchens were being supplied with. Water sellers almost never came during the dry season.

When we reached the entrance of the great hall, a herald got ready to announce us.

"Her Royal Majesty Beatrice Ighomena Accra, Her Royal Highness Imotentenya Aria Accra and His Royal Highness Lucky Accra," he yelled as the room fell into silence and low bows.

Mama and the Prince moved to the other end of the hall to the head table through a parted sea of people and tables.

I turned to the side to see David standing at the corner of the room, diligently surveying his surroundings. All of a sudden, Avery slid up next to him and whispered in his ear. They immediately left through one of the back doors. A shiver went down my spine. I had told David what I heard Avery and Oluwade discussing, but he must not have taken it to heart. Sure, he said something about increased security and checks on Oluwade, but he could have been saying all that to appease me.

I stopped thinking about it as I came to my seat that was next to Mama's: right where the king was supposed to be.

Mama gestured with her hands and everyone scampered to their seats at the tables. With the lowered heads I saw Oluwade at a table in the far corner of the room seated with his wife and two daughters. The shortest one was wiping her forehead with a silk handkerchief, that looked similar to the one Oluwade gave me. I took it that she was his youngest daughter whom he had been talking to me about.

"Honoured guests," Mama began, standing regally. "Thank you for attending this wake for my husband, our late King." A silence descended across the room. "Though these

270

times may seem dark and uncertain, today we are here to celebrate the life of a great man and beloved man."

A mourning song was sung by some singers as candles were lit in front of the floor to ceiling picture of the King. When I used to look at him, I saw my father, a powerful man who I was in awe of. Now I only felt pity for a man who had no idea what was going on in his household only until the end.

It was my turn to light a candle. I knelt down beside Mama who looked up at the picture with a faraway expression on her eyes. I reached out to take her hands when the doors to the grand hall flew open. We all turned to see a bunch of guards marching in led by Chief Agoto. We stood up immediately and the Prince charged down the hall.

"What is the meaning of this?" he yelled as four guards rallied behind him. Chief Agoto looked unfazed and just stared plainly at the prince. "Answer me, man!"

"Your Majesty," Agoto began, "Your Highness, forgive the force but it is an urgent matter that requires the queen's attention."

Everyone in the room turned to mama who just straightened up and followed Chief Agoto back out of the room. A flurry of murmurs arose as I looked at the prince whose eyes were fixed solely on the door mama had gone through, which she came back through only a moment later.

I walked towards her, my heels pinching my toes and when I got closer, I saw her downcast eyes and ashen face.

"I'm afraid a distressing matter has been brought to my attention", she said, meeting everyone's eyes as most of them got up in silence. Her eyes met mine, with the same look she had given when I found out the prince was my father. I heard thunder roll outside and a cold came over my stomach.

"The Northern States have attacked Xavia."